The Musical Ascent of Herman Being

A How-to Novel

NEWLY REVISED

Robert Danziger
CALIFORNIA STATE UNIVERSITY, STANISLAUS

Jordan Press
Modesto, California 1995

First Printing 1985
Second Printing 1988, Revised Edition
Third Printing 1995, Newly Revised Edition

Library of Congress Catalog Card Number 95-75889
ISBN 0-9613427-8-1

Art & Design: Vickie Eden & Jonathan Retz

Published by and available from:
JORDAN PRESS
620 Sycamore Avenue
Modesto, CA 95354

PHONE 209 571-2030

To My Family - The Whole Bunch
Old and New

Herman Being had never been afraid of birthdays. He was almost disappointed that he wasn't losing his hair. He had been prepared to be bald. He wouldn't have combed the hair From the side of his head over the top like Lyall Pratt. Pratt was the personnel manager at Metro Data Processing where Herman worked. He always appeared to be balancing something on his head, and held it at a slight tilt. A breeze or sudden move was enough to cause the entire arrangement to slide off and dangle ludicrously over his left ear.

Herman had offered some candid advice. He told Lyall that he looked better without the cover-up. Lyall told him to mind his own business. Then last week when Herman had his twenty-seventh birthday, Lyall had introduced him to the circle game: You make a reasonable estimate of how long you might expect to live; you draw that many circles on a sheet of paper and then you go back and draw a line through the ones you've used up.

Herman had always considered himself well adjusted, secure and particularly opposed to the obsessive cult of youth worship. He considered it futile and stupid. But this circle game had given him the creeps. Pratt had really got him, the rat.

Last week Herman was just a kid, with lots of potential and a promising future. Suddenly the time for potential was past. Why wasn't he given more responsibility and allowed to do the more challenging work he was capable of. He deserved a better position, a better salary. And how about his personal life? Twenty-seven and single. He was sure he would have been married by now. He wasn't the single type. He had been close to marriage twice, but neither girl had been really right. Maybe it was him. Maybe it was unreasonable to hold out for something really right. Herman was feeling old and depressed.

Even the little things about life had started to bother him. Well, maybe they weren't so little, and the whole truth was that he had felt a dissatisfaction for some time before the circle game. It was hard to put his finger on it, but there was something about the quality of life aside from career and social questions. Despite his recent complaints, he did make a good salary he enjoyed his work and he was healthy - yet something was definitely missing. He sensed a shallowness in his existence. Somewhere inside him an aesthetic capacity was drying up for lack of use.

The idea of becoming more involved with classical music had been forming vaguely in his mind. He was attracted by the idea that this music was uplifting and that some claimed to be enraptured or transformed by it. Since he had only a haphazard exposure, he wasn't sure how much of this to believe. Would he be limited by his background? He had studied guitar for a while as a kid, but it hadn't worked out and the lessons ended after a short time, so he was essentially untrained.

One thing he knew for sure was that he was out growing rock music. Arriving home from work, out of habit, he had turned on the top forty station. *Drive-in Baby* was on. It was a big hit - number one this week. It told of the singer's unrequited love for the waitress at a drive-in fried chicken place. "Look at me, twenty seven, staring senility in the face, and I'm listening to *Drive-in Baby*. I'm too old for this junk." Now that he thought of it, he had never identified completely with rock music. The language, for one thing, wasn't really his own. Even as a teenager he had never called anyone "baby." When he was nine his mother had given him a smack for saying "ain't" and he hadn't said it since.

On the other hand, all of the above notwithstanding, he couldn't deny that the song had appeal. Musically, something about it got through to him. "Well, hell," he though, "Why just sit here ruminating? Herman Being is not a slave to habit. If I want to listen to a classier variety of music I'll just do it. At least I'll give it a try." He dialed to one of New York's "fine music stations" and caught a suave announcer finishing a serene commercial for a candlelit restaurant. "What a relief from blaring, hysterical commercials about close-out waterbed sales." The announcer finished describing the restaurant's specialty of the house (with crabmeat and sautéed mushrooms) and it was time for "Starlight Concert."

Relaxing in his chair, Herman was glowingly optimistic. "This has been long overdue." Beethoven's *Symphony Number Seven* was announced. He found the subtle sound a welcome change - soothing. After five minutes he didn't think he felt particularly uplifted. "Patience," he counseled himself. "This is heavy stuff. Give it a chance." Ten minutes later he was fairly certain that he was not enraptured or transported. Bored would be more accurate - greatly bored.

He looked at his watch. He had been bored for the better part of sixteen minutes. The second movement was still moaning along, and the oily-voiced announcer had forecast four movements. It was fine to be open minded, but how long was he supposed to sit there, bored, before admitting that this was not working? He figured that sixteen minutes out of Herman Being's life was enough. The experiment was over! He dialed back to one of the pop stations and just happened to catch the final strains of *Drive-in Baby.* The familiar curve of the melody gave him chills of satisfaction.

He had tried it and he didn't like it. No sense kidding himself. He was not one of those people that could act like they enjoyed something when they really didn't. Thinking it over, he concluded that the failure must have been due to one of three things:

1. There was a gap in his education. He didn't understand what was going on, therefore, he didn't appreciate it.

2. De gustibus non est disputandem. Different strokes for different folks. Some people were naturally high class and sensitive to classical music, while others were low class, insensitive, with common taste. (In light of this, he de-

cided that it would be just as well not to mention his experiment to anyone.)

3. The whole thing was a put-on. The Emperor's new clothes. Nobody really liked this music. They were all bored, but wouldn't admit it, afraid to be dumped into the second category of number two above. The whole thing made him more depressed than ever. So depressed, in fact, that he almost considered turning on the television. He was low, but not that low.

Several months ago he had been watching TV for lack of anything better to do, and he was struck by the feeling that his brain was turning to fodder. He didn't know what fodder was, but he didn't like it. Since then he had not allowed himself to watch TV just to kill time. He was depressed, but not defeated. He read for a while and went to bed early.

A few weeks later Herman's Aunt Irene called. She was a librarian at New York University and lived a few blocks from Herman in Greenwich Village. She was going to a concert with a graduate student she'd become friendly with at the university - a girl named Jean. She had an extra ticket, and thought that Herman might like to join them. Herman had graduated From NYU a few years ago, and she felt that they might have something in common. Herman thought that he might find some experiences to share with a pleasant young graduate student, though he wasn't sure that he would agree with his Aunt on important qualities in concert partners.

He thought back on his unsuccessful experience with Beethoven's *Seventh.* "Well, it's worth another shot. Maybe a live exposure will make the difference." Inwardly he wasn't sure how much his willingness to give it another try was real, and how much was due to curiosity about

Jean.

The evening began with an early dinner at Captain Joe's Sea Food House. To Herman's surprise, while a bit on the shy side at first, Jean turned out to be bright and not unattractive - altogether comely, in fact, with resplendent long hair. Both she and Herman were somewhat embarrassed as it became obvious that Aunt Irene had to be thinking of setting them up. Herman felt he could bear the affront, offered as it was in so well chosen a form. Cheered by the thought that things could have been far worse, he found the food and conversation very pleasant.

By the time the waiter came to clear away the wreck of empty shells, apprehension had given way to buoyant cordiality all around. They decided to put off dessert until after the concert - maybe stop in Little Italy at a late night cafe. Herman picked up the tab, and a short taxi ride brought them to the concert hall in plenty of time.

Lights played on the fountain at Lincoln Center. Even the crazy junkpile of a modern sculpture in the entranceway struck Herman as tolerable....interesting. Herman thought about what a pleasant overall experience this concert-going is. Aunt Irene handed him his ticket. "Even this," he thought, "could be just a bit of paper. Instead it's finely printed in two subtle colors - and the quality of the card stock...," he rubbed his thumb on the ticket, "it's like a tall, slim playing card." And the people - nicely dressed, clean, relaxed. Those with the wild outfits on seemed fashionably eccentric. Even the humble nose was treated to a random array of fine perfumes. Architecture - eighty foot ceilings, marble, polished brass, huge chandeliers, the aura of culture.

It turned out that Jean was working on a master's degree in music. She said that the surroundings reminded her of a paper she was working on. The point was that for centuries this kind of experience belonged exclusively to the tiniest fraction of society - the king in his court. Today it's available to practically everyone. She recalled writing, "In western society today, in a cultural sense, each citizen is a king without a crown." The point was not lost on Herman as he assumed his throne, three in from the aisle in the dress circle.

House lights dimmed, the oboe intoned the tuning note. The conductor swept in to applause. Musicians in black and white. Light reflected in golden varnished spruce of violas and maple scrolls of the cellos. Silver flutes, ebony clarinets.

Herman relished the first sounds of the orchestra. Here in the hall the balance was perfect. He felt as well as heard the basses and timpani. The string tone was tactile. He imagined that if he hung out his tongue he would taste it, but decided against the experiment in consideration for Aunt Irene.

So far things were as usual. He had always enjoyed the first ten minutes of a concert. After that, except for occasional, especially colorful moments, the novelty of the sound wore off. After twenty minutes, his spirits sinking, he felt the familiar weight of boredom.

Three rows ahead a bald-headed older man was nodding off to sleep. "How foolish," thought Herman. "Ten bucks a ticket and the old guy takes a nap. What a waste...On the other hand, at least he's getting some sleep. The rest of us are sitting here counting off movements. Ten bucks a ticket and, the truth is, I'm sitting here waiting for it to be over."

He wondered, as he looked around, how many of his fellow concert-goers would actually prefer a fifteen or twenty minute concert to the usual two hour marathon.

"That would be just about right.   Captain Joe's Sea Food House, a refreshing fifteen minute concert, and then on to the cafe for an eclair and a cup of cappuccino."

With these thoughts, drowsiness overtook Herman and he drifted into a light doze.

A loud scream jolted him awake.   "Where am I? - I'm at a concert - I fell asleep - Who screamed? Was it me?" His heart was pounding.   Everyone was looking at the empty seat where the bald-headed man had been.   It appears that the poor old guy had awakened with a startled yell and fallen off his seat. His mortified wife was helping him up. His eyes were like saucers. So were Herman's. "Thank God it wasn't me! Thank God it wasn't me!" It was ten minutes before Herman's pulse slowed. He was sweating. He did not doze off again.

An odd event occurred toward the end of the concert. The last piece was a large scale classical work. Two thirds of the way through the last movement, the composer had inserted some deceptively final-sounding chords; a sort of false conclusion after which the piece was to continue to the real conclusion five minutes later. However, at this evening's performance, the audience had begun to applaud after the false ending. The conductor had stood poised, hoping for the applause to abate. Some of the bass fiddle players waved their bows in the air to signal that all was not over, but half of the audience had obliviously pulled on their coats and raced up the aisles and out the doors. It appeared that for a good part of those attending, the evening's main objective was to beat the crowd out and get a cab.

When the chaos subsided, the orchestra continued with a somewhat sheepish rendition of the last five minutes of the piece. The remaining half of the audience applauded politely and slunk out.

On the way out, a big, spongy-looking guy about Herman's age recognized Jean and Aunt Irene. Waving his way through the crowd, he greeted them with kisses and an elaborate embrace. Jean introduced him as Duncan Latren, a fellow grad student in music at NYU. Aunt Irene had known him for years from the library. The conversation quickly moved to the peculiar events at the end of the performance.

Duncan was disgusted. "Here we are in what's supposed to be a cultured, sophisticated city, and half of the audience just demonstrated that they are totally ignorant and insensitive; completely incapable of following the composer's clearest intentions. First of all, it was a piece from the standard repertoire, therefore, everyone should have known it well enough to realize that it had not ended. Second, even if someone had not known the piece, it should have been obvious that it couldn't end at the deceptive chords: they were in the dominant key, and proper form demands that the piece end in the tonic. And third, even if a listener were so totally stupid and ignorant that he didn't know the piece and knew nothing of keys or form or anything, he should still have been able to feel that the piece was not over, if only by innate sensitivity."

Aunt Irene said, "Bulldinky." Duncan had been spending too much time with his nose in a textbook. Big deal! So the audience made a mistake. So what? She didn't come to listen to forms and tonic keys. Dominant, shmominant! She didn't come to keep score or to second guess the composer - and if she'd ever heard that piece before she certainly didn't remember it. She just came to relax and enjoy the sounds. She liked to think her own thoughts during the concert and, if you wanted to know the truth, she thought Duncan was turning into an egghead with his big deal master's degree. Don't forget, the stupid, insensitive people Duncan was raving about formed the vast majority of the public, and without their support there wouldn't be any concerts!

Eyes turn expectantly to Herman. He would like to say something conciliatory to both sides. He, too, thought Duncan was somewhat full of beans, but he wasn't anxious to admit it since this would put him in the stupid insensitive camp. On the other hand, he really expected more out of a concert than Aunt Irene did. Enjoying the sounds and being left to his own thoughts was nice for a few minutes, but his dozing off and rude awakening had been one of the most harrowing experiences of his life.

He decided to attempt a subtle change of subject. "I think I'll try the cafe mocha with my eclair tonight. Should we get a cab, or wait for the bus?"

In the next few days Herman's mind returned frequently to the events of that evening. He was tempted to call Jean and suggest another get together - maybe this time without his aunt. But he lost his nerve at the chilling recollection of his dozing-off episode. What did a guy in the computer business have in common with a musician anyway? Lately his sincere attempts at musical involvement had been extraordinary flops. She was bound to discover his deficiency. Better not to take the chance. Too bad - he would really like to see her again. He tried to remember how she looked in her summer dress, in the cafe, eating a cannoli.

The phone rang. It was Jean. She wondered if Herman might give her some advice on how to computerize some data she was working with. Against his better judgment, he jumped at the opportunity. A get-together was arranged at Aunt Irene's place.

He arrived half an hour early, with mixed feelings. If only he didn't feel so insecure about this music business, he would be delighted at the prospect of seeing Jean again. He decided to put the time to good use. Determined to bring all his intelligence to bear on the problem, he approached the piano. He would compose a piece himself, right from scratch. That way he'd discover the guiding principles of music first hand. Why didn't he think of this before? Don't underestimate the resourcefulness of H. Being under pressure!

He would start with something simple and pleasant. By trial and error, note by note, Herman's fingers sought a pleasant sounding chord. So far, so good. He had one - a tremendous start! He never heard a nicer chord. Now for a little rhythm and he was off. He established a regular pattern, and "Being's First" was under way.

A few minutes later he was forced to acknowledge a problem. His piece wasn't going anywhere. Nothing was happening. What started out sounding pleasant and soothing had become predictable and boring - the thing Herman hated above all in music. H. Being would not write monotonous music! He would start over.

This piece would be unpredictable. Adopting his most mercurial expression, Herman played random notes: high-low, long-short, soft-loud. No one would ever discern a pattern in this. His new piece had a familiar sound - reminiscent of a number of seemingly legitimate twentieth-century art music compositions he had suffered through. This did not console him as he admitted another gigantic failure in his experimental approach to understanding music. He hated both his compositions equally. A feeling of despair filled Herman as he heard Jean arriving.

Later in the evening his spirits revived due to the influence of Jean's cheerful personality, and because he proved to be of real help with the computer problem. He outlined a scheme to organize her data. She admired his knowledge and ability. In a flash of inspiration he hit on a tactic for his own problem. If she could ask him for help in his field, why couldn't he do the same? He would confess his frustration with music and risk appearing an ignorant fool. It was a desperate attempt.

The description of his sour relationship with music ended in recounting his latest fizzler of an experiment earlier that evening. He went so far as to attempt to demonstrate his two abominable compositions.

To his great relief, she was not reduced to hysterics, though she did agree that they were two of the most obnoxious compositions imaginable. She was touched by his openness, and said she would love to try and help him.

She consoled Herman with the idea that his experiment came very close to an important musical concept. The same elements could be found in all arts and, for that matter, in life, since the one, to be meaningful, must relate to the other.

The elements were essentially two, and they were opposed: repetition and contrast, unity and variety, conflict and resolution, tension and relaxation, the expected and the surprise. These pairs of words express different aspects of the same general opposing forces. All effective music uses these forces in some balance. Although totally opposite in almost every other respect, Herman's creations shared the woeful distinction of using one of the two opposing elements to the exclusion of the other.

Herman might have been more successful if he had tried to maintain a balance between the two. A composer must have the ability to sustain this equilibrium; to make us feel comfortable by establishing certain patterns, creating expectations. Then the opposing force is brought to bear, our expectations are defied, the patterns are varied, countered or extended - contrast, surprise, conflict. Familiar patterns reemerge and the conflict is resolved.

This design can be observed on a miniature level in a simple melody within a few measures, or in a great symphony on a tremendous scale where the listener feels conflicts and resolutions of a magnitude that can only be compared to the workings of life itself.

Jean played some familiar pieces on the piano and Herman was amazed that, with his attention directed, he heard clear examples of unity and variety, expectation and surprise.

She explained that this was the simplification of a complex and subtle process. She was not at all certain that composers consciously thought of it, and doubted that it would help if they did. But, as a listener, she found it fascinating to discover these contrasting elements. The intellect was engaged and a conscious kind of understanding could emerge, both of the musical process in general and of the construction of the particular piece.

This reminded Jean of a lecture she had heard in which Leonard Bernstein discussed Beethoven, the giant among composers, and what it was, particularly, that made his music great. Bernstein's contention was that Beethoven's melodic writing was not in itself remarkable. Other composers could be said to have a greater purely melodic gift.

Jean recalled the specific example Bernstein had used and she played it for Herman on the piano.

It was the first theme from the slow movement of Beethoven's *Seventh Symphony*, a hauntingly moving funeral march. When Jean played the melody alone, however, Herman was astonished to realize that it consisted entirely of one note, slowly intoned again and again - twelve times before rising two steps, and then only to continue the repetitive tolling - essentially a one note melody.

In his use of harmony, rhythm, form, orchestration, or any of the individual elements that constitute the whole of music, neither do we find Beethoven's powers clearly superior to those of his colleagues. What did make Beethoven great was his ability to put these elements together in carefully, meticulously balanced patterns of tension and resolution in a way, Bernstein maintained, that would strike the listener as unexpected, surprising, some times shocking, but at the same time... inevitable.

Something was bothering Herman. He had heard this dirgelike, one note melody before. Now he remembered. It was this same Beethoven's *Seventh* that he had compared to *Drive-in Baby* in his radio experiment. In fact it was in this very movement that boredom had caused him to conclude that he was insensitive to classical music. "Just my luck," he thought to himself. "Beethoven gets stuck on one note just when I happen to be running my experiment. No wonder I gave up."

But there was a difference now. One note or not, he found the music more expressive, mournful and beautiful. Was this because, as Jean had explained, his attention was focused and his intellect engaged? Possibly - or maybe partially. Somehow he suspected that there was another force at work here, something that had yet to be discovered.

In any event, what Jean had provided seemed to make sense. He wondered if this new awareness would prove helpful in practice. He would need time to judge. Meanwhile, it had been an encouraging evening from all points of view.

A position as operations manager opened up at Metro Data Processing. It was just what Herman had been waiting for; better salary, more responsibility, and the kind of work he wanted. He turned in his application.

When Herman had come to work for Metro, it had been a progressive company, but the last few years had brought a change in leadership. Since, in his present job, he was working on estimates and bids, Herman was aware of a tendency to cut corners on quality, and to pad customer's bills. The practice of fixing bids particularly bothered him. As there was no shortage of work, companies able to handle certain big jobs would agree to take turns. They consulted one another before submitting bids, and the company coming in low would actually charge more than the job was worth.

For the new position, applicants were required to

submit a statement of goals. Without dwelling on ethical questions, Herman expressed his view that the company concentrating on quality work at a fair price would come out ahead in the long run, and still generate a comfortable profit. He foresaw dangers in that:

1. Customers would inevitably discover inflated charges.

2. Fixed prices would encourage new competition to enter the field offering lower prices and better work, discrediting the existing firms.

It would be several weeks before the selection process concluded and the new operations manager was announced. Of those that applied, Herman was obviously the best qualified and most capable. Why then, when he ran into one of the big shots in the hall, did he have the feeling that he was getting the small hello. Maybe it was just his imagination.

In the weeks that followed, Herman thought often of Jean, and wondered if they'd ever get together again. So when his annual invitation to attend alumni day came in the mail, even though in the past he had easily ignored the idea, he found himself inspired by a powerful urge to visit the old campus. He started a letter to his aunt, hinting for her to arrange a get together with Jean. Becoming angry at his cowardly approach, he wrote to Jean directly, saying that he would like to see her.

She wrote back promptly that she would look forward to it. Since she would like to show him around the new music library, she suggested that they meet there. Herman was bothered by the elation he felt in anticipation of alumni day. He had a talk with himself. "Take it easy! Big deal! She only said she'd show you a library. You've seen libraries before, haven't you? What are you, in love after seeing this girl twice?" It wasn't much help.

On alumni day, Herman took a bus to the university. He tried to appear casual as he arrived at the new music library forty minutes early. He was surprised to find Jean already at the assigned meeting place. Shy smiles from both parties, followed by a hesitant attempt at a handshake in which they only succeeded in fumbling with each other's fingers.

The music library was interesting. Jean took him to the listening area - her favorite place. As they looked over the thousands of neatly catalogued recordings, Herman saw the great appreciation, almost wonder, with which Jean regarded the collection. She thought it was wonderful to have access to countless hours of the finest music of centuries. In addition to the usual carrels with stereo phones for individual listening, there were some pleasant, comfortably furnished small listening rooms with complete stereo systems including speakers.

Jean said, "Actually these rooms are intended for groups, but they're never all full and I like listening in here better than using headphones. There's something I don't like as well about the headphones, even though you can actually hear more detail with them. It sounds silly, but I don't like the feeling that I'm the only one who can hear what I'm listening to, especially if I'm really enjoying it. When I'm in one of the listening rooms, other students come in to say hello, and even though it might detract from my concentration, I like to share the music with someone." Herman thought he understood. It occurred to him that this urge to share an enjoyable musical experience is one of our few completely unselfish inclinations.

While Herman looked around one of the listening rooms, Jean went to the main desk and returned in a few minutes with a new CD. "Here's a new recording of Tchaikowsky's *Nutcracker.* Should we put it on?"

"Sure, let's try it. It doesn't make sense to stand here and just look at all this great equipment."

The sound was phenomenal. It seemed to Herman that he was hearing the music not only through his ears, but through his whole skin. He marveled at the ring of the triangle and wondered how such a clear, metallic sound could emit from this plastic disc. He imagined that he would stare into a digital groove and find a microscopic strip of silver. And he was overcome with the music itself. He had heard the *Nutcracker* before, but it had never affected him like this. Jean said, "It's not fashionable around here to listen to Tchaikowsky, especially a piece that's as well known as this one, but it's still one of my favorites. I have no idea when I heard the *Nutcracker* for the first time - I was probably too young to remember. I guess that's why it's inconceivable to me that someone actually sat down and made it up out of nothing. It just seems so perfectly natural, as though it always existed, like the moon or the stars."

There was a loud knock, and Duncan Latren's grinning face appeared in the door window. Entering, he greeted Jean as though he hadn't seen her in fifty years, with his elaborate hug and kiss. Shaking hands with Herman, he asked, "Do my ears deceive me, or are we listening to the inimitable, slushy sound of the *Dance of the Sugar Plum*

Fairies? What could have possibly inspired you to listen to this? Are we perhaps reliving fondly remembered days as little kiddies?"

"Duncan is well known for his dislike of Tchaikowsky," explained Jean. "He loves to argue, but I never get anywhere with him. I've learned to ignore his cheesy insults."

"Dislike?" continued Duncan, "Dislike is inaccurate. I abhor the work of your simpering psychopath." Jean explained to Herman that Duncan was the music critic of the student newspaper, and, in her opinion, took his work too seriously. He was an avid fault finder. Name a composer, and a list of shortcomings would roll from his tongue. "He does like Mozart though."

"Yes, even you, Jean dear, with your shameless poor taste, must recognize the superiority of the one perfect composer."

"Well, I think it's unnecessary to talk about 'superiority' of any of the great masters, but, yes, we do agree that Mozart is a wonderful composer."

Although the conversation was more or less directed at him, Herman was beginning to feel a bit left out, not wanting to venture opinions on something he knew nothing about, or even to ask questions which would only serve to flaunt his ignorance.

Jean wanted to show Herman where they kept the tapes. Duncan said he would wait for them, and they left him in the listening room, flourishing gestures in a parody of over-passionate conducting. As they walked alone now, Herman commented, "Kind of a strange guy. Do you know him very well?"

"No, not really very well."

"Does he greet everyone with a big hug and kiss like that?"

"I haven't really noticed. Why do you ask?"

"Well, it just seems a little unusual for someone you don't know very well to grab you and kiss you every time your paths cross, which must be fairly often around here."

"Herman!," she said, half-trying to disguise her amusement. "I should really be annoyed with you. It almost sounds like some sort of jealousy...Would you be happy if I told you I think he's a harmless, puffed-up ass? Did it bother you when he greeted your Aunt Irene the same way? Really! I'll have to watch out for you if that's the way you think. Besides, I don't think Duncan is interested in girls - and he wouldn't get any encouragement from me if he was."

Herman found himself both embarrassed and stimulated. "Well, I was just asking. After all, it's not so far fetched. Two musicians would share important interests."

"Not in this case. Duncan can be entertaining, but I don't have much respect for his musical opinions. Let's try an experiment. We'll test his musical judgment." Jean checked out a cassette and they returned to the listening room. Duncan had already taken off the Tchaikowsky. Jean said that she was putting on a piece for strings and horns by Duncan's favorite - Mozart.

They listened to the first movement. Duncan, appearing transported, said that he had to leave. But he thanked Jean for allowing him to cleanse himself in this glorious music so typical of Mozart's genius.

As soon as Duncan was gone, Herman asked Jean, "O.K., so what's the trick?"

"First, tell me what you thought of the music."

"I wasn't crazy about it, even though it did have a pleasant sort of classical sound. It seemed dull, and didn't make much sense. But that's a common reaction for me - that's my problem. Besides, I was prejudiced against it because I was expecting some sort of trap. I think you probably found this piece by some third-rate old bozo, and said it was Mozart. Didn't your mother ever tell you it's not nice to tell a falsehood?"

"Well, I've never been so insulted. I did not tell a falsehood. It is Mozart!"

She explained that they had listened to the first movement of Mozart's *Musical Joke*. Mozart had been struggling to make ends meet, as he did all his life, and he was frustrated by the easy success inferior composers found by pandering to popular taste. The *Musical Joke* was written as a parody. In it, Mozart tried purposely to do everything poorly: subtle mistakes in harmony, lack of imagination, prosaic melody or total lack of it, incompetent treatment of form - just plain bad writing. In the first movement, which Duncan had heard, Mozart had kept his parody subtle, but, as they listened to the other movements, things became more ludicrous and sometimes very comical.

Jean said, "Someone like Duncan who prides himself on a critical ear should certainly have picked up Mozart's intentions, even in the beginning. I'm glad he left before the obvious parts. It would have been mean to make him admit that he'd been fooled. You see? This all proves that I have more in common with you than with Duncan. So are you still jealous that I 'share important interests' with him?"

"Well, no...but I think I'm still jealous about sharing the hugs and kisses."

Herman was walking her home late that night. When they were still several blocks from the dorm, he surprised Jean by thanking her for a lovely day, saying that they really had to do it again...good night, and walking briskly away, leaving her astonished at his sudden departure.

Before she had gone a block farther, however, she noticed someone walking toward her from the opposite direction. It was Herman. At first he appeared not to notice her, and then recognition flashed across his face, and he called, "Jean! How have you been?" and gave her a big hello hug and kiss. It really might have been very much in Duncan's style, except that it tended to drag on a bit.

Now Herman was worried. It was true that he had felt attracted toward classical music on his own, before meeting Jean, but it was also true that his attempts at musical involvement had been, at best, unsuccessful. He had been spending more time with Jean, and their relationship was in danger of becoming serious. But she was still a musician, and he could not realistically imagine an intimacy that his present state of ignorance and confusion wouldn't strain.

He held off calling her for several weeks, telling himself that he needed time to find out how he felt before getting in any deeper. He even began to get together with a few girls he had been seeing before Jean. He found it relaxing not to feel constantly on the verge of exposing his ignorance or insensitivity. Was it, as he hoped, because the music issue was eliminated, or was it because he was simply not as intensely involved as he had been with Jean. At first he wasn't sure if this was good or bad, but then these easy relationships began to seem mindless. Relieved at having gotten away from Jean, he felt at the same time strongly drawn back. These opposing inclinations left him drained and unhappy. Aunt Irene cautiously asked him how things were going in a way that led him to think that Jean might have been asking about him, but he restrained any indication that he recognized this, and was then haunted by the feeling that he had thrown away his last chance at reconciliation.

He was spending Thursday night staring into the dark above his bed, as he had done regularly in the weeks since he had last seen Jean, when he finally gave in. She was obviously the right girl for him. The musical problem was annoying, but relatively unimportant. He would have to find a way to deal with it. He would call Jean in the morning and make amends. A great relief overtook him, and he slept soundly for the first time in a week.

So soundly, in fact, that he woke up late and didn't have time to call her in his rush to get to work. He intended to call later in the morning, but what he found at work caused him to put it off.

A decision had been reached on the position of operations manager. A memo thanked him for his application, and informed him that the position would be filled by Lyall Pratt, formerly personnel manager. Herman couldn't believe it. Pratt, in addition to being a bad tempered jerk, didn't know a thing about operations. He was a phony, a yes man. Things were bad enough before. How would the company survive? But that was not all.

Pratt had always been jealous of Herman's ability His first move in his new position of power was to send a memo to Herman, telling him he was being transferred into the supply unit. "What? Is he kidding?" Herman couldn't go to supply - it was a dead end. This was a deliberate insult. They were trying to get rid of him. So, this is what happens when you tell them what they don't want to hear, the miserable bastards. He had until Monday to let them know his decision.

Herman knew that if he went to supply and kept his mouth shut, in a year or two they might let him back into operations. If he refused the transfer, he'd be fired and other companies would not fall all over each other to hire a trouble-maker. He was tempted to turn in his resignation then and there, but he knew that this was just what Pratt wanted. He decided to take the weekend to try and think of a more satisfying exit.

He didn't call Jean. He didn't forget, but there was no sense kidding himself, he was upset and would be until he knew what he was going to do. Friday night and Saturday he paced and thought. The more he thought, the more anger burned inside. By Saturday evening he had settled down enough to begin planning a course of action. He went to bed exhausted.

He woke to what sounded like a soft knocking on his door. The clock said 5:30 in the morning. Did he imagine the knocking? There it was again. He put on his bathrobe, opened the door a crack and peeked out. It was Jean, bundled up in an overcoat, holding a very small brown paper bag. On her face was a combined expression of fear, hope and helpless desperation.

She said, "Ah.....sorry.....were you asleep?"

"Ah.....Well yeah, I guess I was sort of dozing there.
....but that's okay. Ah.....Come on in." She came in and
stood next to the door, looking at a loss for what was to
come next. Finally -

"I realize it's sort of early. Ah.....but I thought I
would bring you something.....and I decided not to wait.
....and I hope you're not mad at me." She hesitantly
opened up the wrinkled bag, and Herman saw what looked
to be three eggs.

"Ah...It's three eggs," she said. "I thought maybe you
would want an omelet....."

"Sure.....I love omelets.....My stomach doesn't usually
get up for a while though. Ah.....Why don't you take off
your coat and have a seat?"

"Oh, I'm not sure.....I left in a rush and, well.....I'm
still wearing my nightgown."

"Oh.....Well, that's okay.....It's still early to be really
dressed up. I mean, look at me, for instance. I usually
don't even consider really getting dressed until about seven
or so.....six-thirty the earliest. Look, if you're hungry you
can make an omelet for yourself."

"I'm not hungry yet either - just sort of cold and tired."

"Yeah, me too. You want to just rest for a while, until
we get hungry?"

"Sure.....Where?"

"Well.....I have a bed."

"Oh.....Is there room for both of us?"

"Sure.....Come take a look." They went to view the bed.

Jean asked, "Should we go on top or under the covers?"

"It would be warmer under the covers."

"Right. Are you mad at me?"

"I'm definitely not mad at you. If this is a dream, I hope it's going to be a long one."

Later in the morning they had burnt toast, burnt omelets and orange juice. Jean said, "I have a confession. The eggs were just an excuse in case I lost my nerve. I actually came to seduce you."

"You don't say. Now, just a minute here. I admit to having been a little on the cautious side, but let's keep the facts straight. You may have shown up here in your night-gown and got under the covers with me, but from there on, I seduced you."

"Well, maybe so, but if you're such a hot lover, how come you haven't called me for three weeks?"

Herman explained his problems of the last weeks. For years he had been socially and professionally secure and couldn't find the right girl. Now, he found the right girl, and everything else had collapsed. "Last night, I decided to quit my job; so what am I supposed to say? I'm an unemployed ignoramus, marry me? The truth is that I'll probably ask you soon, even if things don't get better, but I need some time either to straighten things out, or to get used to feeling like an unemployed ignoramus."

"If you asked me today, I'd say yes."

"You're not making this easy."

"Well, it's not so easy for me either. I've been offered an assistantship in Idaho."

"Idaho?"

"Idaho! So what happens if I turn down my big chance in Idaho, and then you decide you're too much of an unemployed ignoramus to ask me?"

"When do you have to let Idaho know?"

"In about a month."

"Okay. In one month we'll have a meeting and take a vote. Agreed?"

"Agreed."

So the question of yes Jean or no Jean was resolved - it was yes Jean. Now he had a month to put himself back on his feet. First he had to work out his professional crisis, and second he was determined to have one more shot at this music business. He would have a busy month.

In mulling over his situation at Metro, he realized that his troubles started when he warned the company that if things didn't change, new competition was bound to enter the field. Things seemed to be falling into place: they chose not to change, and he was out of a job. In a sense he was being challenged. If he really believed in his theory and had the nerve to follow it through, his path was clear: he was to become the competition.

At first it sounded great, but then the details - one man couldn't maintain an operation by himself. He wouldn't need to start big, but he would need something; a small shop and office space, a part-time secretary, and a handful of the right people would do it. He had respect within the business, and the right connections. He had managed over the years to save 12 thousand dollars. Yesterday it seemed like a lot; today it seemed like very little.

One thing kept him from dropping the whole idea: he had decided that he was finished with being somebody's employee. Never again did he want to depend on someone else's approval to make his living. He wrote out his two-week notice. His last two weeks on salary. ..two weeks in which to do a lot of talking to people. He would never have guessed that a turbulent event was about to cut his career at Metro even shorter.

On the musical front he had some ideas, but here he felt the need for advice. Although they hadn't seen much of each other in recent years, Ben Walden had been a familiar figure in Herman's childhood. He was a longtime friend of Aunt Irene's, and a musician. It dawned on Herman that here was someone who might be able to help him. Monday night, he called Ben and was told to come right over.

Ben lived alone in Brooklyn, in a small, old, one story brick house with a red tin roof. You might expect to look in the window and see the three bears sitting around eating porridge. Four afternoons a week Ben gave piano lessons at home. His students were mostly kids, and some adults. He pulled in about eight thousand a year this way, and managed to live on it.

His place was full of books, music, cigar smoke, old bus depot furniture, lots of patched-together second hand stereo equipment, and on the walls hung large, amorphous abstract oil paintings in various shades of dark green. The paintings, along with some volumes of poetry and musical compositions, were original works of Ben himself.

Except for teaching, his time was spent either creating art, music and literature, or experiencing the great works of others. That he did sell some of his creations from time to time was strictly of secondary importance; his involvement in the arts, an involvement totally devoid of the usual social associations, was an essential fact of his existence.

They had a long conversation in which Herman unfolded his situation in great detail. Before he finished, hunger had driven them to a Chinese restaurant. They had winter-melon soup, Cantonese lobster, and roast pork fried rice. Herman wanted to try the "Special Oriental Fantasy Dessert," but Ben insisted on ordering plain vanilla ice cream.

They walked back to Ben's place and Herman ended his story with a plan to become musically literate through the study of music. With the help of a book on musical instruments and the record of *Peter and the Wolf* he had decided to take up the bassoon. He realized that it would take time and dedication, but he thought he could do it. He wanted to know what Ben thought of this.

"To be honest, Herm, it sounds like a pretty crazy idea. You might learn to burp some notes out on the bassoon, but that's no guarantee that you'll understand or appreciate music any better."

"Well, what would you suggest?"

"I suppose I could lend you some books. I have quite a few here that are supposed to teach music appreciation. Some of them are really well done. They talk about instruments, voices, forms, styles, lives of the composers, historical background. Some have color plates of related visual arts; some come with a set of recordings. Most of them focus on specific pieces and give you analysis to follow."

"Great! Do you think it will work for me?"

"No."

"No? Why the hell not?"

"Well, I don't want to sound arrogant or discouraging, but these books are great for music lovers - people who are already initiated and want to learn things about music. I don't think they have what a guy like you really needs. What you want to know is how you get to love music. These books don't really deal with that."

Ben went over to the bookshelf, grabbed a paperback and thumbed through. "Here's an example. Now this is one of the best books on music appreciation: *What to Listen for in Music,* by the great American composer Aaron Copland." Ben read from the book:

> The only thing one can do for the listener is to point out what actually exists in the music itself and reasonably to explain the wherefore and why of the matter. The listener must do the rest.

"But what is the rest? That's what you want to know, and he doesn't tell you. None of them do!"

Looking a little confused, Herman said, "Well so far you offer to lend me a bunch of books, and then tell me they won't do any good. We're off to a great start "

"Relax," said Ben, "I'm just thinking out loud. We'll come up with something."

"This listening process is turning out to be a real mystery. Does anyone understand it? Do you?"

"Yeah, I guess I understand it "..

"Well, let me in on it, will ya? This is no time to be shy. I'm desperate. You think I came all the way to Brooklyn just for plain vanilla ice cream?"

"I'm trying to find a way to help you without scaring you off. I wasn't sure how serious you were about this. I have some pretty unorthodox ideas on this subject, and you might think I was a little off."

"So what? I've known you were a little off for twenty years now, and that didn't keep me from coming to you. Being a little off is your most endearing quality. Let's stop worrying about your credibility, and tell me the secret. Either it will work or it won't."

"All right. There really is a secret, you know. Let's go back to that great experiment you did with the pop song and Beethoven's *Seventh.* What was the name of that tune again?"

"You know what it was - You just want to hear me say it again so you can have another big chuckle."

"Oh yeah; I remember now; *Drive-in Baby,* wasn't it? Now, we could get into trouble here because we don't have a good, common word for the positive response to music. 'Enjoyment' isn't good enough. We don't 'enjoy' being moved to deep sadness by a requiem. When someone finds his or her existence made more meaningful by a deeply felt musical experience, it's not enough to say he or she 'enjoyed' it. It's not always beautiful; it doesn't always make us happy; it isn't always relaxing. Sometimes we respond to ugliness or excitement. So, for the sake of clarity, we'll use the word 'affect' with an 'a'. When music gets through to us, or moves us, or communicates emotion, we'll say it's 'affective.' Now, how many times had you heard *Drive-in Baby* when this occurred?"

"I don't know for sure. I don't even remember the first time I heard it. It was number one that week, and I had just gradually become aware of it. I'd say I'd heard it about eight times before that."

Ben picked up a pad and pencil. "Okay, here's a chart of your reaction to *Drive-in Baby*

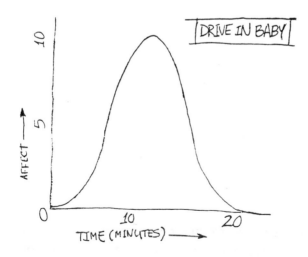

"Up and down is 'affect' and left to right is 'time'. It's about a two minute song, and you say you heard it about eight times: that would give us about 16 minutes. By that time you loved it; it blew your little computer expert's mind, right?"

"I'll overlook your feeble sarcasm and agree for the sake of argument".

"And you managed to sit through two movements of Beethoven's *Seventh*. That gives us roughly the same amount of time: about sixteen minutes.   And you were underwhelmed by this."

"Significantly underwhelmed."

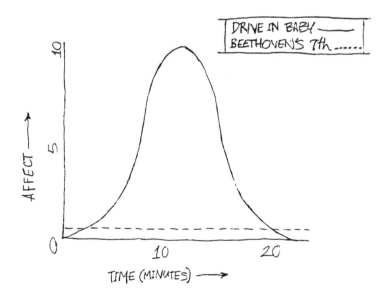

"So, both sides got sixteen minutes and Beethoven lost

fair and square, right?"

"Right."

"Wrong! You're not accounting for the key element: repetition. You listened to the two-minute pop tune eight times. Beethoven's *Seventh* is probably forty minutes long. To really do this experiment you would have had to listen to it an equal number of times. Forty minutes times eight would give you well over five hours."

"Five hours? That's not an experiment, that's an ordeal!"

"Well, it might start out that way, but if you survived it, my contention is that the chart would look like this:"

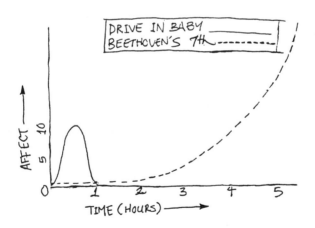

"Let's take a look at what we've got to work with so far. We've established that you do respond to pop music"

"I can't deny it, embarrassing as it is."

"Don't be too embarrassed. If you didn't like any music at all, then we'd be in trouble. At least we have a basic sensibility to work from. Have you ever read Darwin's *Descent of Man*?'

"I've heard of it, but I've never read it."

Ben found the book on the shelf. "I'll read something to you:

> As neither the enjoyment nor the capacity of producing musical notes is of the least use to man in reference to his daily habits of life, they must be ranked among the most mysterious with which he is endowed. They are present, though, in very rude conditions, in men of all races, even the most savage.....

That last category is where you fit in. What we're trying to establish is that we don't need to teach you to appreciate music; you have that instinctively. We only need to extend that capacity; to sustain, deepen and intensify.

"But," said Herman, "that's only true if you ignore the difference between popular and classical music."

"Okay, so what is the difference?"

"I'm supposed to have the questions; you're supposed to have the answers."

"As far as I'm concerned, the essential significant difference is length. Pop tunes are always short - average about two and a half minutes. Classical pieces are usually much longer. More than anything else, this makes popular music popular and classical music relatively unpopular.

"The top forty system is based on repetition. You didn't remember the first time you heard *Drive-in Baby*, but the more you heard it, the more you liked it. The record promoters are sure as hell aware of this. They don't expect a tune to make it to the top on one exposure; they push for repetition. And it works great; it makes money - which is more than you can say for classical music.

"Meanwhile the program director at the 'fine music station' is doing just the opposite; spacing out the repertoire. God forbid a symphony should be played twice in the same month."

Herman said, "I would never have thought that length is the main difference."

"Nobody thinks so. Nobody thinks!," said Ben. "There's plenty of evidence. Every few months some joker rips off another tune from the classics and comes up with a big hit. It's been going on ever since the radio was invented. Tchaikowsky's *Piano Concerto* becomes *Tonight We Love*; Borodin's tunes from the *String Quartet* and the *Polovetsian Dances* become *So This is My Beloved* and *Stranger in Paradise*. A Minuet by Bach becomes *Lover's Concerto*; his *Jesu, Joy of Man's Desiring* becomes *Joy*. Both Beethoven's *Fifth* and Mozart's *G Minor Symphony* have been raped repeatedly this way. We could make a long list. Most of the time they just arrange the tune in a popular idiom and then - the important thing - They cut it down to a few minutes."

Herman said, "Suppose I argued that change of idiom was just as important as length in making these songs popular."

"All right, let me give you evidence against that." Ben put on a CD. "Ever hear this before?"

"Sure," said Herman, "It's the *Theme from Elvira Madigan*. Beautiful. I love it. Did they steal this from a classical composer?"

"Yes and no. It's the second movement of Mozart's *C Major Piano Concerto*. But in this case the pop version was identical to the original - piano and orchestra, just as Mozart wrote it two hundred years ago. The sole difference is length; the popular version was shortened. Proof that this is the important element."

Herman asked, "So if it's been around in this same version for two hundred · years, why didn't it become popular a long time ago?"

"That's what's so absurd about this whole phenomenon! It has very little to do with the musical material. It's the circumstances, the format, the way the music is presented that makes the difference. Of course it's very beautiful, but no more beautiful than a hundred other pieces that Mozart wrote, each in its own way. But this piece, probably because of its particular obscurity, was chosen as background music for the movie, *Elvira Madigan*.

"By the end of the film it would have become somewhat familiar through repetition. People might have asked, 'What is this fantastic music?' Whether they knew it as Mozart or *Elvira Madigan*, the results were the same; increased demand leading to increased exposure. Soon people who had never seen the movie would recognize it, and before long - a big hit for Mozart - two hundred years too late!

"The irony of it kills me. This is the 21st of Mozart's 26 piano concertos. They were written at the end of his tragically short life when he was desperate to establish financial independence. It didn't work. He went deeper into debt, his health deteriorated and he died, leaving his wife and children, at the age of thirty five.

"He had started composing before he was five, probably the greatest natural genius the world has ever known, and he was buried in an unmarked pauper's grave. Why couldn't a success like *Elvira Madigan* have happened sooner? It could have freed him from the struggle that drained his health and energy. The music didn't change; neither did the way we hear it. It didn't become gradually more popular over the two hundred years. It went from obscurity to approbation only because of the circumstance of presentation. It wasn't even intentional.

"In a few years you'll be thirty-five yourself. By then you'll be a great music lover, and you'll have experienced the immensity of his genius. Then you'll begin to understand the depth of this tragedy. And it was shameful ignorance of the process by which we respond to music that dealt Mozart only half a life."

The conversation had taken place over the beautiful

lonely sound of the concerto. Now, as they sat quietly, the music continued and it seemed to Herman that it reached more deeply than it had before.

The movement ended and, after a brief silence, Herman looked at his watch. "Wow, look at the time. I'm not prepared to spend the night out here in the sticks. I hope they don't close the tunnel. Can I come back for more of this later in the week?"

Ben said, "Now that we got started here, you damn well better come back. I'll do some thinking about a definite plan of action. I think this is good for both of us."

After his long night of art and philosophy, Herman was ready to deal with the problem of making a living. Of his twelve thousand in savings, he put aside two thousand to live on for a while. He knew that this did not leave him enough to start his own business. He needed two things to make Being Computer Service a reality; the right people and more capital.

He knew some good people in the computer business, and he made a list of the best of these. After discussing his idea with three of them at the top of the list, two seemed very interested and were giving it some serious thought. They represented a balance of strengths; they seemed to be compatible, and each thought they could probably scrape together some money. It wouldn't be a great deal of money and they would need time to work on it. They agreed to meet in a week for more discussion.

It was Wednesday. Herman had a week and a half left on salary. He arranged to meet Ben after work at an Italian clam bar on Sixth Avenue. Herman had an order of baked clams oreganato, a side order of spaghetti with garlic and olive oil, salad and Italian bread. Ben had salad, bread, and two dozen cherrystones on the half shell. They split a pitcher of beer.

After eating, they began walking to Herman's place, a few blocks away. "Where were we when we left off?" Ben asked.

Herman said, "I think you were getting ready to unveil the secret of the listening process. The way you were building your case, I don't need Sherlock Holmes to tell me what it's going to be."

"So what do you think it is?"

"Well, we've established that I respond to pop music; that this response depends on repeated listening; and that pop and classical music aren't as essentially different as I thought. The logical conclusion would be: apply the re-peated listening procedure to classical music; and that's the secret."

Ben said, "Sounds too simple, doesn't it?"

"It sure does."

"Well then, why the hell didn't you think of it your self, wise guy? Or any of those windbags that write six hundred page books about listening to music and never mention it?"

"Who's arguing?" said Herman. "It makes sense to me.

But isn't it just sort of common sense? And those books must suggest listening to a piece more than once."

"You're a worthy student, you feisty little devil. I can see that rhetoric and sweeping generalizations are not going to convince you. Good, good. This is a subtle point - a crucial point - and I deserve to be challenged on it.

"You're right; most people would agree that it's probably good to know a piece well, and that repeated listening is an obvious way to do it. And most music appreciation books do warn that just reading or talking about music won't take the place of listening. But what I'm after is not the natural, passive, common sense inclination to get to know a piece. How about the idea that after the first time through, if you don't like a piece, there's no need to listen again because you'd only hate it even more? That's common sense too. But this is not at all what I'm proposing.

"You see, when you hear a piece, let's say six times, not necessarily one right after the other, but within a reasonable time, changes occur in your perception that are unexpected. The first few times through, you'll have little or no hint of these changes. After several repetitions you're astonished that a degree of affectivity has crept in. It's a revelation! Where was it hiding? How could you have missed it the first time? It comes as a matter of wonder.

"I've been aware of this for more than thirty years; and every time it works for me I'm amazed. I expect it to work, and yet each time it works unexpectedly.

"On the one hand, it's a very simple idea and it proves itself every time you use it. On the other hand, it requires the denial of a very strong natural tendency: to form a judgment on first hearing. After all these years it still takes an effort of will to resist the feeling that I know a piece after I've heard it once. Each time the Devil talks to me: 'What, again? Why again? What will you hear the next time that you didn't hear the first time? Don't be a fool! You heard it - you know it!'

"But it's not true. I don't know the piece, after one hearing, any better than I know a person after shaking hands and saying howdy-do. Sure, I've encountered it, but to know it requires repetition.

"Every once in a while I'll be having a conversation about music, and I try to make a quick point about the marvel of repeated listening, sort of half assuming that other people must have experienced and recognized it. The reaction is usually: 'Ah yes, repeated listening; a valuable tool. I indulge in it myself...often.' And then in the next breath this same guy will deliver an opinion, as if carved in stone, of a piece he heard once, didn't like, and dismissed forever as unworthy. If he really understood, he would know that forming a judgment on first hearing is a total contradiction of the real concept of repeated listening."

By now they had reached Herman's apartment. "You know what? Trying to talk you into this is dumb. We need to get on with the practical part of this experiment so you can learn from your own experience. What kind of equipment have you got around here for listening to music?" Herman pointed to his twenty year old Zenith portable phonograph that Grandma had given him when he graduated from junior high school.

"That's what I was afraid of," said Ben.

"I just put a new needle in a few years ago," said Herman.

"I'll bet you had a hard time finding one. Those fancy needles that flip from 78 to LP are hard to come by these days. I brought along a record for testing equipment, but I don't think I want to risk putting it on. I can tell just by looking at it that we're not in for any sonic thrills with this thing."

"Well.., I've thought about getting some new stuff." (This was true, but before he quit his job.) "Would I be able to get anything decent for a thousand bucks?"

"If you know what to look for, you can get everything you need for a lot less than that."

"Okay, I'll grab my checkbook and let's see if we can find a stereo discount store that's still open."

By the time they arrived at the store Ben had convinced Herman that having hopelessly outdated stereo equipment and a meager record collection was actually a circumstance of particular good fortune.

"What you've got to understand is that we've entered a new era in recorded sound. In the last few years two developments have revolutionized the industry. First, digital recording and then the compact disk."

Ben explained that the digital process reduces live sound to a digital code with the tremendous advantage over the older "analog" recording, that the code can be transferred From one medium to another, the studio master recording to a compact disk, for instance, with absolutely no deterioration of accuracy or quality. In addition, the digital code exists independent of the material carrying it and is there-fore never wedded to record surface noise or tape hiss, as in even the most sophisticated analog recordings.

"Sure," said Herman, "I understand the digital process From my work. But what's the big deal with the compact disks? They look like cute little records."

"Oh, more than cute," said Ben. "Beautiful, exquisite, treasure-like, large futuristic coins. They play seventy minutes on only one side - never need flipping over, easy to store, easy to handle. But the real excitement is that the digital code is permanently sealed below the surface of the disk. It's read by a laser beam - nothing physical ever touches the coded material, therefore, no wear, no dust, no fingerprints, no tape hiss, no insidious sound of the stylus being dragged primitively through a tiny vinyl toboggan run. Just awesome, absolute silence and then breathtaking, undistorted sound. I'm really jealous. I've had to nurse and protect a constantly deteriorating collection of LPs and you get to start from scratch with these fantastic new CDs that will always sound as pristine as when you first play them."

Herman started looking at the all-in-one combination amplifier, tuner, cassette, CD player and speakers. Ben steered him away from this. He maintained that with separate components Herman would get better quality and have the option of changing and updating parts of the sys-tem.

An exception to this rule was the receiver; a combina-tion of a tuner, needed to pick up radio signals, and an amplifier. For reasons nobody seemed to understand, it was cheaper to buy a good quality receiver than either an amplifier or a tuner separately. They found one on sale with forty watts per channel, which Ben said would be plenty, for $89 - less than half the $290 list price.

Ben found some highly rated speakers on sale because they were demos - $99 for a pair - the usual price for one. Next they found a CD player, sale price $139 with a feature called "oversampling' which Ben liked as it made a subtle but worthwhile improvement in the quality of sound. Herman would have been easily lured to higher and higher priced models as the salesman expounded the need for remote controls, programmability, and various other gadgets and deluxe features, but Ben was against them. "We should stick to simple, basic, good quality equipment. If something doesn't have a direct effect on the sound that comes out, stay away from it. These labor savings models that flash signals and do everything automatically turn out to be an expensive pain in the neck. Fifty bucks more for this and fifty more for that, then you find out that you don't use the extra features and every added light, switch, whistle and bell is something else to break down or go out of adjustment."

Although they had everything that they really needed, Herman found a good deal on a cassette deck. Things were costing less than he had expected and he reasoned that with the cassette deck he could tape FM stereo programs. Ben had brought along a cassette recording of the Mozart *Clarinet Concerto* for equipment testing. The clarinet has such a pure, straight sound that any flutter or wow in a tape player would show up right away.

Ben had also brought along a compact disk recording of Brahms' *Symphony #3*." He liked to use the third movement for testing and comparing equipment. Now they listened to the components together to insure compatibility.

The system sounded wonderful and the bill came to $417 - less than Herman had expected, but he forced himself to act sort of hesitant and to make comments about what a lot of money it was and how maybe he should think it over for a while, until the salesman offered the whole deal for $400.

They made two trips to carry the new equipment up to Herman's apartment. "You know, Herm, much as I disdain your vulgar ability to spend four hundred bucks in an evening, I have to admit that I'm having a ball with this stuff. I love all these plastic bags and molded styrofoam and neat factory-coiled cords. Smells great, doesn't it?"

Since they had been using the CD of the Brahms as a test recording throughout the evening - all the starts and stops probably added up to about four or five run throughs- it dawned on Herman that he was unintentionally being provided with his first opportunity for exploration of the repeated listening process. It had occurred to him because he found the last few times much more appealing than the first few.

The equipment was finally ready, and they sat on the couch for the final test. As the now familiar sound of the Brahms filled the room, Herman felt an ecstatic glow inhabit his spirit. It was a feeling that he would never forget.

He somehow didn't feel up to verbalizing his revelation. Instead he said to Ben, "I just had a disturbing thought. If your plan works, what's going to keep me From renouncing normal life to become an art crazed derelict like you?"

"Nothing," said Ben, "if you're lucky, and you have the nerve for it."

Somehow word had gotten around Metro Data Processing that Herman was planning to go into business for himself, and that he might take some of the company's best employees and maybe some customers with him. It had been Lyall Pratt's idea to force Herman out. So now that it might backfire, the people in charge were mad as hell, and Pratt was getting it from all sides.

It was the first day of Herman's last week at work when Jean came hurrying into the shop looking for him. She spoke to Pratt, who told her that Herman was out on a job and wouldn't be back for several hours. She said that she couldn't wait, but she would like to leave a note for him.

She wrote:

Dear Herman,

Something has come up. The select choir from school is going on a 3-week concert tour of Europe. One of the altos has mono and they asked me if I'd fill in. I think I ought to go.

Right now I feel like I'd rather stay here and be with you, but it's a rare opportunity and truthfully, I've been feeling very stupid about throwing myself at you last weekend. The least I can do is give you time to make up your mind without interference from me.

I'm supposed to leave tomorrow at noon. Call me ☺

Love,
Jean

She put the note in an envelope and gave it to Pratt, asking him if he could please make sure Herman got it because it was very important. When she left, Pratt opened the envelope, read the note, and threw it in the wastebasket.

Herman noticed an atmosphere of tension when he returned to the office. Pratt, appearing even more keyed up than usual, waited until there were a few other men in the office, then he told Herman that a girl had been in looking for him. Herman was suspicious since Pratt had been acting more belligerent than usual, and lately hadn't spoken to him at all. His first thought was that it might have been Jean. He asked what she looked like.

Pratt said, "Nice - medium height, great body, long brown hair. She told me all about what you did this weekend. She said you didn't do too well so I offered my services. We went in the back room and I gave her a taste of what a real man is like"

A part of Herman's conscious knew that he had been purposely set up for this, and that it was no accident that Pratt had positioned himself next to the desk where there was a gun kept in the drawer. But that part of Herman's mind was not in control. He was moving toward Pratt to beat the hell out of him, and Pratt was reaching into the drawer screaming, "You touch me and I'll blow your God damned head off!"

The first shot hit Herman in the leg, just before he grabbed Pratt. The second and third shots went wild. The gun fell on the floor as Herman pounded Pratt senseless. As Herman moved away, Pratt began to crawl toward the gun. Herman grabbed a fire extinguisher from the wall and buried Pratt in a whoosh of white foam. The pain in Herman's thigh was increasing. He limped out of the building and took a cab to a nearby hospital.

The doctor who removed the bullet was very complimentary. He said Herman really knew how to take a shot - no real damage - just a hole. He would have to stay overnight. His folks came to the hospital and so did the police. They took his story and left. He tried Jean several times and got no answer before the nurse gave him a shot to make him sleep.

He woke up just before lunch the next day. They gave him crutches, instructions on caring for his hole, and told him he could leave later in the afternoon. He would have to stay off his leg as much as possible for at least a few days.

Arriving home in the evening, he tried Jean again; still no answer. It made him uneasy. Why had she tried to find him at work? What had she really told Pratt? What was behind that crack about the weekend? On the other hand, there was probably a simple explanation. Jean was probably just at the library; she never spent much time in her room. He decided to call her in the middle of the night when she was sure to be in. It would wake her up, but at least he'd put his mind to rest. Two thirty A.M. and Jean did not answer. He fought the cold, empty feeling creeping over him, his mind racing to find reasons that she might not be home. Was it because of the events of the last few days that he felt so desperate to find her?

It occurred to him to call someone from school who might know where she is. Duncan Latren - at 2:30 in the morning? So what. The hell with it. He called anyway. No answer. What was going on here? He didn't sleep. At 7:00 A.M. he called Aunt Irene, hoping she might know something.

Yes, Duncan was on tour with the select choir in Europe, but Jean was not in select choir. She would see what she could find out. At 9:30 she called Herman. Her friends in the music department had solved the mystery. Jean had gone to Europe as a last minute replacement. The grip of tension began to loosen. Still......no word? No message? Pratt! There must have been a message, that bastard! He breathed deeply and relaxed. The pain in his thigh actually felt pleasant.

By noon, Aunt Irene had a copy of the choir's itinerary. Herman sent a wire to Jean in Cologne:

NEVER GOT YOUR MESSAGE

CALL ME COLLECT

LOVE HERMAN

Jean called late that night and they talked for an hour and ten minutes. The call ran up his phone bill by ninety-seven dollars.

Herman called Ben the next day. "Hey, Herm! I've been trying to get you. I think I've got a plan worked out here. Where've you been?"

"It's a long story. I need some help. My mother was just here and she left the fridgy full of ready-to-eat yummies. How about if you bring your plan over here and we have a feast?"

"You talked me into it "

An hour and a half later Ben rang Herman's bell. "What's with the crutches? Is that the long story?"

"Yeah. somebody shot me."

"Ha, ha," said Ben.

"I knew you'd say that. I'm not kidding. I got caught in a gunfight without a gun."

"Well, in that case you didn't come out too badly. I guess this guy wasn't much of a marksman."

"Yeah, well he had difficulty aiming with my thumb in his eye."

Ben said, "This witty banter is entertaining as hell, but somehow I'm not getting a clear idea of what happened. Why don't you start from the beginning"

"Okay, let me just put this stuff in the oven to heat up."

"I don't know if I can eat anything," said Ben "shootings ruin my appetite.... What is it?"

"My Mom's chicken paprikash with dumplings."

"Well, maybe I'll just taste it to be polite."

Herman related the events of the past few days while they ate, and while Ben's appetite failed miserably to exhibit any proof of its delicate nature. The story ended with Jean's phone call from Europe.

"So, what'd you talk about for an hour and ten minutes besides getting shot?

"Getting married," said Herman.

"Oh, whose idea was that?"

"This time it was mine."

"I thought you were giving yourself a month to decide."

"Yeah, well when I couldn't find her for a couple of days, I changed my mind."

"Well, I'm not gonna talk you out of it.   I think it sounds great.   Does this mean you can give up learning to love music?"

"Hell no.   I'm more determined than ever.   And this is the perfect time to do it.   I'm on sick leave for my last week of work.   In a few days I get together again with these people who are interested in forming a partnership to see if we can come up with enough money to put the new business together.   Aside from that, Jean won't be back for almost two weeks, so I can give your secret method a real test.   Besides, my leg hurts and music soothes the savage thigh."

"Great! I've been finding this very interesting.   I'd be disappointed if you gave up now.   God, I love dumplings. I thought they were extinct."

"Well, this batch is extinct anyway.   You just ate the last one.   So how about getting back to the secret method?"

Ben said, "As long as you brought it up, I have to tell

you that my conscience has been bothering me about calling this my secret method. See, I do know that other people are always bumping into it. Every once in a while I'll be reading something and there it is: a clear reference to my own discovery. This fascinates me, and I sort of collect them. In fact, I brought some examples for you. Here, read this."

Ben pulled a CD out of an old shopping bag he had brought with him, and pointed out a paragraph on the liner notes.

This movement (movement III of *Suite #1, op. 43*), Tchaikowsky told his patroness, was the one she was certain to like best when she be came fully familiar with the suite, for "I wrote it with real warmth!

"You see?" said Ben, " 'Fully familiar!' Tchaikowsky was aware of the effect of repeated listening. So how come then, he would write a piece and when it wasn't greeted with wild enthusiasm after the first performance, he would time and again be crushed and driven to the brink of suicide?" Another CD emerged from the shopping bag.

"Here, look at this one. This is Brahms' *G Minor Sextet*. At first, as usual, it wasn't appreciated. But, as usual, those who persevered through repeated performances found a great masterpiece revealed. Elizabeth Von Herzogenberg was an old friend of Brahms. Here's what she wrote about one repeat performance she went to:

...I heard much that had been hidden before. It

is like having a flashlight turned on first one place, then another, all the discoveries going to enrich the precious inner store.

You see? A perfect description of the repeated listening phenomenon. Read it again; it's beautiful.

"Here's another one - Edward Downes, the music critic, is writing about *Kreisleriana*, a group of piano pieces by Robert Schumann:

Its concealed riches, its many levels of meaning, do not reveal themselves all at once - or at a second or third hearing - even to professional musicians.

Now Ben pulled three books out of the bag. The first was *Questions About Music* by the American composer Roger Sessions. Ben read to Herman:

...it should be obvious that one cannot pretend to even begin to know a piece of music on the basis of anything but repeatedly listening to it with full and undivided attention.

"Well," said Herman, "This was written fairly recently.

If Sessions is a respected figure in the musical world, maybe now that he's explained it people will start to catch on.

"Don't bet on it. Here, look at this. The great English composer William Byrd tried to tell us almost four centuries ago in the preface to his "Psalms, Songs and Sonnets of 1611:

> ...a song that is well and artificially made cannot be well perceived nor understood at first hearing, but the oftner you shall heare it, the better cause of liking you will discover: and commonly that song is best esteemed with which our ears are most acquainted.

"And here's my favorite reference to my secret method. I saved this for last. It's from a book that nobody ever reads called *Friends and Fiddlers*. Start from here:

> Leo is fifty-five, a practicing physician. He neither plays nor sings, he cannot read a note - but where is music, there goes Leo on the run. It has not always been thus, with him. "When I was forty," he told me, "I asked a friend, 'what is this music you talk about and spend money to hear?' The people I like best all go to concerts and come out feeling better than when they went in. How can I join this club? What is the password and how may I learn it?"

His friend told him to go to concerts, "But not just any concert. Go this way: Choose some special piece, say, the 'Fifth Symphony' of Beethoven, and every time you see it on the billboard, go and hear it. And see what happens."

The first time he heard the "Fifth Symphony," Leo was bored. He was bored the second time, and the third. But he is a persistent fellow, and he went again. This time he recognized a tune. "The andante tune," he told me. "It was terribly exciting, waiting for the cellos to do that tune. They were beginning to play it, and I knew what was coming next...And the fifth time I heard it, I wanted to cry."

"See?" said Ben. "There it is! For fifty years the secret method has been sitting on page 72 of this little book. Do you think it changed anyone's life? No! Because even Mrs. Bowen who wrote it didn't really appreciate it. The phenomenal thing is that today it's easier and more practical. We don't have to wait around for the same piece to show up on various concerts; we have recordings."

"I think I'm getting confused," said Herman. "First you tell me about this great secret method and then you shower me with all this evidence to prove that it's not a secret method."

"I just didn't want to leave you with the impression that I think I'm the only person who ever noticed this. It's like I said - other people are always bumping into it. The difference is that I use it all the time, consciously; as a fantastic practical device. But you're right: Too much talk and not enough action."

"Yeah, let's have the plan already." Ben pulled the Sunday Times out of his bag, found the list of Philharmonic subscription concerts, and pointed to a program a little more than two weeks away:

Romeo and Juliet- Overture Fantasy - Tchaikowsky

Piano Concerto, D Minor, #20 - Mozart

Kindertotenlieder - Mahler

"The plan is for you to go to this concert. If we're successful, it should be a life enriching experience. This will give us a few weeks to get ready. I'll copy out the program; you get on the phone and reserve a ticket - reserve two if you want to take Jean."

"I'll reserve three," said Herman. "We'll all go!"

"No, thanks, Herm. I don't go to concerts much. I'd just as soon avoid the strain."

"Well, that's a hell of a weird attitude for somebody who's supposed to be teaching me to love music! What strain?"

"I don't know... I don't want to make a big issue out of it. I guess under the circumstances I should attempt an explanation. It's a little embarrassing. It seems I'm getting too sensitive. These composers and this music, some of it is pretty powerful if you really open yourself up to it. It can wring your emotions. With me, the effect seems to get stronger as I get older.

"Like that program you're going to. That's strong stuff. There isn't a piece on there that I would submit myself to listen to in public. Hell, I wouldn't listen to that stuff on the telephone, unless I was by myself.

"How'd you like to be Joe Shmoe sitting casually at a concert, and in the next seat some old coot is sobbing with joy, tears running down his face? I could be locked up! The last concert I went to was Handel's *Messiah*. Everybody's heard the *Messiah* a million times. I thought I'd just go sit through it again. Well, I knew I was in trouble from the beginning, but I thought that I'd be okay if I tried not to listen. Then I felt this part coming. I tried to think of something else, but it comes like thunder. Maybe you know the part - the whole chorus sings:

AND HIS NAME SHALL BE CALLED -

WONDERFUL! COUNSELOR!

THE MIGHTY GOD -

THE EVERLASTING FATHER -

THE PRINCE OF PEACE!

"I broke up, and it took all my effort to keep from making a complete spectacle of myself. I left at intermission, thinking about how stupid I was to put myself through that. What good is it to go to a concert where my choices are:

A) Don't listen

B) Make a scene

C) Try not to listen and make a scene anyway.

Lately I prefer listening alone where my ecstasy is less embarrassing."

Herman said, "We could use a sensitivity exchange. You've got too much, and I haven't got enough."

"You don't know anything about how much you've got," said Ben, "until you give yourself a chance. So reserve those tickets, and I'll go out and buy some CDs."

"Hang on. I'll order the tickets, and then I'll limp along with you. The record store is right down the block."

Before they left for the record store, Ben reached into the old shopping bag one more time, and brought out a Copy of the *Opus* catalogue. He explained to Herman that everyone who listens to music should know about this paperback record, tape and CD guide. It's updated monthly and lists complete information on every record, tape and CD currently available.

They studied it for a while, choosing among various recordings of the works that would be presented at the concert.

Herman was surprised that Ben generally preferred American orchestras and performers. Ben denied that it was patriotic favoritism; he said that in recent years the best music in the world is made in the United States.

The prices are listed in the back of the catalogue, and Herman did some comparing to find the best bargains. Ben said that there are no real bargains in recordings. The newest, best sounding recordings with the finest performers cost more and are usually worth the higher price.

On the way back from the record store Herman checked his mailbox. There was a letter from a law office. Herman recognized the names of the lawyers that represented Metro. The firm's client, Lyall Pratt, was bringing a lawsuit against Herman for assault and battery.

"He's suing me?! The bastard shot me! I don't believe it!" For the rest of the night the subject switched away from music and focused instead on where to find a good lawyer.

The next few days Herman spent in meetings: Meetings with his new lawyer and meetings with his potential new partners.   Herman's father had recommended his own lawyer; he had known him for fifty years; said he was a great guy - a tiger in the courtroom.   Herman went to his office above a shoe store on Sixth Avenue and 14th Street.

Everything in the office was old - especially the lawyer. No receptionist, no secretary; just old chairs, an old desk, some old files and an old lawyer in a baggy suit; Marvin Grossman.

As Herman related the events in question, he could have sworn that Grossman had fallen asleep.   But when Herman had finished, the lawyer opened his eyes and asked a string of questions that did indicate a grasp of the situation.   He asked for the names of the witnesses and some information about them.   Herman wanted to know what he should be doing. Grossman said that, aside from staying away from fire extinguishers, he shouldn't do anything.

"Look," he said, "you got the Perry Mason of Sixth Avenue working for you. Go home and don't worry." Herman said, "Yeah, that's what they told Sacco and Vanzetti." He considered asking Grossman if he had handled that case, but decided against it. He really didn't want to hear the answer.

Neither did his meeting about the new business serve to lift his spirits. The other two potential partners could each get together about ten thousand dollars to match Herman's if they really scratched, but to quit their jobs and at the same time commit the money (they would have to mortgage everything down to the doghouse to come up with it) was just too much of a risk. Even if they were crazy enough to try it, no matter how they figured, 30 thousand was not enough to really set up the new company. Borrowing was out. Without a business record, the banks wouldn't talk to them; and even if they could get a loan, high interest would suck off any possibility of survival.

For a few minutes Herman mourned the passing of his neat fantasies: Two-color business cards, an office with small trees in pots, a company owned "Mr. Coffee" machine... Then he proposed a different approach. Since he was out of a job anyway, he would make the rounds - talk to people - let them know he was in business. He would buy an old beater of a station wagon for a few hundred bucks and work out of his apartment. Whatever work he could scare up he would do himself. The other two would keep their money and their jobs. When Herman got more work than he could handle himself, they would work nights with him. And when they got more work than they could handle this way, then they would talk about money and a full time partnership. What it lacked in glamour was made up in practicality. They agreed it was worth a try.

He had been somewhat concerned, with life becoming complex and demands on his time more pressing, that he would be hard put to continue pursuing Ben's plan, determined though he was to follow it. In fact, whatever it was that had originally attracted him to an involvement with art music, that need, seemed not to diminish but to grow stronger along with the pressure of his business and legal struggles. He could attribute some of this to the obvious benefit of simply taking his mind off his problems for a while, but it was much more than just this.

As he prepared to begin the listening part of the plan in earnest, he found a few basic questions that he thought ought to be answered. He decided to make another pilgrimage to the little house in Brooklyn. "I'm not trying to be argumentative," began Herman. "I know there's a good answer to this question - I sort of feel it - but I'd like to be able to understand it consciously. We've decided that pop music and classical music aren't as different as they appear to be; they're not opposites and they share many similarities. Aren't there any important differences between them? Because if there aren't, it would make sense to stick with pop music since it's handier and much more practical."

"Okay," Ben answered, "we have established that the essential important difference between the two is length; classical generally longer. Well, there's another aspect to this. Extending a musical concept over a span of time adds something more than just minutes. With length, comes depth. A twenty minute symphonic poem is not the same as eight or ten short pieces strung together. Think of it in terms of literature. The short story and the novel share many characteristics aside from length, right? And it might be fine and very pleasant to read short stories one after the other. But this won't offer the fullness, the capacity for deepest involvement that you find in a great novel. "It's possible to have positive, valid experiences with both types of music. But, when you look for something beyond this, something greater. when the capacity for deep involvement is in question, then we find a difference between the two types.

"I have a book here somewhere; *Popular Music* by John Rublowsky. Let me see if I can find this one passage. ...Here, he's talking about the nature of pop music:

> We do not come here for heaven storming reve-lations nor to hear a message for the ages. ...communication is the sole aim of popular music. It does not aspire to educate, to inspire, to broaden, to uplift - all it wants to do, baby, is be friends with you!"

"Well put, right? But how about those of us who don't shrink from education or inspiration; who don't mind being broadened or uplifted? Some of us feel that revelation through art is a positive idea and that the concept of a message for the ages is fascinating. For us the choice is clear. The scope of classical music allows all of this and at the same time, just as popular music, it can still be 'friends with you.' Ultimately it's up to us to choose our 'friends.'"

"Okay," Herman said, "I can accept that, and as I said, I'm drawn toward classical music because, somehow, I expect to find these things. But it sounds like we're dealing with a factor that goes beyond just the length of the piece. There are some short classical pieces, aren't there?"

"Sure, Schubert songs for example - hundreds. Most of them fantastic masterpieces, and all just about the same length as a rock song."

"Aha!" said Herman. "So we're not just talking about length, are we? We're talking about quality. So tell me, what makes one piece better or deeper than another? And while you're at it, you might as well go right back and explain the essential musical phenomenon from the beginning. Jean helped me with this one evening by explaining tension and resolution. It really helped. I've been able to recognize these elements in everything I listen to, but it doesn't really go back far enough. I want to know what it is about these combinations of vibrations that people find appealing. A simple question: Why do we like music?"

"Oh, sure! Simple question! Why don't you throw in some other simple questions about the nature of infinity, the origin of the universe and the soul of man?"

"I've done it!" shouted Herman. "The oracle is confounded!"

"Like hell. The oracle is hungry. Let's check in at the deli - and then I'll show you who's confounded."

When Herman was a kid, Ben used to take him to Cohen's Delicatessen. It hadn't changed. The same faded sign had been hanging on the back wall as long as either of them could remember:

Send a Salami

to your

Boy in the Army

The deli was divided; plain tables for self-service, tables with white tablecloths for waiter service. They sat at a table with a cloth. The waiter, with a faded black bow tie and an off-white towel over his arm, came over.

He said, "So, two tongue sandwiches?" Since neither of them had said anything about tongue, they looked sort of puzzled.

"I hate tongue," said Herman.

"Who asked for tongue?" asked Ben. "We want hot dogs. We always get hot dogs"

"Exactly", said the waiter, "you always get hot dogs, so today you want tongue."

"I hate tongue," said Herman. "It's the only food I hate."

"This tongue you can't hate."

"Well, maybe we'll try it some other day," said Ben. "We really want hot dogs."

"Look, a hot dog is a hot dog."

"Right," said Ben, "and we'll have two each; with mustard and sauerkraut."

"Go ahead, ignore my advice. This kid wants to hate tongue the rest of his life, it's none of my business."

"No need to take it personally," said Ben. "We just happen to want hot dogs."

"Four hot dogs. You win. Forget I mentioned it. What else?"

"Two orders of French fries - well done," said Ben.

"Well done? Roast beef you order well done - French fries, you just order."

Ben said, "Look, I've been coming in here for forty years, and I always get French fries well done. Humor me - just tell the cook, well done."

"The customer is always right."

"You bet. And two bottles of Dr. Brown's cream soda."

"Yes sir - You want the sodas well done, too? Or are you gonna leave that to chance?"

After eating they returned to Ben's place and he picked

up where they had left off.

"Now, before I enlighten you as to how and why music works, and it is with great difficulty that I repress my natural inclination toward modesty, I must tell you that this is not generally understood. If you think you can just pick up any music book and find this, you're wrong. In all my years of study - right up through the master's degree - your basic, simple question was never addressed in a classroom. I know, it sounds incredible, but it's true. If some of us were indelicate enough to raise the question anyway, we were told that since music has always been a part of any society, a universal human phenomenon, and since it has no obvious function, this in itself proves that it satisfies some mysterious inner human need. An artful ruse - it is because it is. Now there's some element of truth here, but it doesn't go far in providing a real explanation.

"Until recently, I have to admit, I wouldn't have been able to do much better myself. I had begun to think it was one of those things that men weren't made to understand. You know who had the answer? Darwin again! In the *Descent of Man*, here, read it yourself.

> ...we may assume that musical tones and rhythms were used by our half human ancestors during the season of courtship, when animals of all kinds are excited not only by love, but by the strong passions of jealousy, rivalry and triumph. From the deeply laid principle of inherited association, musical tones in this case would be likely to call up vaguely and indefinitely the strong emotions of a long past age.

"You see, he presents this by way of making his main point: that speech evolved from music. But it also provides a completely plausible explanation for the emotional appeal of music. Nobody wonders why we like dumplings. Obviously: to sustain life by insuring that we eat. But now we see that music too was a life sustaining force by virtue of its original function in the mating process. To me, this is one hell of a revelation. It's reasonable, it's logical, and it's the product of a great mind "

Herman asked, "So, why don't all musicians know about this?"

"In my own humble mind, I account for it in terms of flagrant ignorance "

"Maybe the musical establishment doesn't like being linked up with raw sex," offered Herman.

"There may be more truth to that than you think. Even today, Darwin is no stranger to controversy. And in addition to being X-rated, his ideas directly conflicted with what the musical scholars were writing on the origin of music; particularly a guy named Herbert Spencer. Read what Darwin says down here in this footnote:

> ...Mr. Spencer comes to an exactly opposite conclusion to that at which I have arrived. He concludes, as did Diderot formerly, that the cadences used in emotional speech afford the foundation from which music has been developed; whilst I conclude that musical notes and rhythms were first acquired

by the male or female progenitors of mankind for the sake of charming the opposite sex. Thus musical tones became firmly associated with some of the strongest passions an animal is capable of feeling...

"It's always been obvious," Ben continued, "that music serves to scratch some sort of itch. The question has been, why we have the itch and where it came from. I'm satisfied that Darwin has the answer. But it only explains the general emotional effect that music conveys. A great deal still remains to understand about the process that produces this effect; the details of how these vibrational patterns take on meaning.

"There's only one place I've ever seen this really dealt with and that's in the book: *Music and Communication* by Terrance McLaughlin. It's only been around for a few years and the truth is, I don't know if it's well known or not; I just stumbled across it in the library. This guy doesn't fool around. He really takes on the whole phenomenon.

"Without this book, a musician can develop a feeling about how music works, but only vaguely; a sort of nebulous understanding, a lot like some aspects of religion. Certain concepts are accepted and referred to freely, based on intuition or faith, without theoretical support. Like the widely accepted idea that great art relates somehow to human existence.

"Well, McLaughlin actually explains the whole process: how music is related to bodily functions like heartbeat and breathing, and to the largest shapes of life - birth and death.

He explains the electrical code that transmits musical patterns to the brain and how the brain compares these with similar patterns from other senses, how the patterns take on meaning as a result. Remember your question about what makes one piece greater than another? Well, here's the answer.

"McLaughlin says that the greatest music, that which is most deeply felt, is analogous to other life patterns on multiple levels. Fantastic! It's not the kind of thing I can sit here and explain in detail. The only way to understand it is to read the book. I'm a believer. But listen, you don't have time for it now. Later on, after you've actually experienced some great music, then it will be more meaningful for you.

"At least now you know: 1. That someone has actually tackled the problem and come up with a theory that follows the musical phenomenon from the beginning to the end, and 2. Where to find the information if you ever need or want it."

Herman found no difficulty in contracting small jobs for himself and his days were getting busier. The facilities and convenience of a bigger operation were missed, but then there were advantages. With no overhead his profit would be higher. More than anything, he loved the feeling of self-reliance and freedom, though in truth he was working longer and harder hours now. In addition, he was lining up some bigger jobs which would involve his prospective partners. The biggest frustration was that he knew of several nice fat contracts that he could practically walk away with - he had been right about this - if only he had the resources to undertake them. Money!

Meanwhile, back on Sixth Avenue, Herman's lawyer had decided to take the offensive. Grossman had convinced Herman to file a countersuit against Lyall Pratt. As a result of this, they were scheduled to meet with two lawyers for Metro Data Processing who were representing Pratt. Pratt himself chose not to attend.

Herman, who had expected some nasty bickering, was surprised at the jolly atmosphere. Everyone seemed so friendly and pleasant. He couldn't help taking this as a good sign. In fact, when they finally got down to business, it started to look pretty good for Herman's side. One of Pratt's lawyers said he had good news:

"We've convinced Mr. Pratt that this unpleasant business has gone far enough. We would be willing to concede that each party has suffered equally and would be agreeable to a mutual withdrawal of claims."

Herman was elated. Maybe he wouldn't end up in jail after all! He really wanted to wrap the damn thing up so that it wasn't still hanging over his head when Jean came back from Europe. When he looked over at his lawyer, his elation evaporated. The Perry Mason of Sixth Avenue seemed to be coming to life. There was a distinct gleam in his eye; he had caught the scent.

He said, "Well, you know, Gentlemen, we didn't start this whole thing, and it has cost my client considerable trouble and expense, but we do appreciate your concern for fairness. On the other hand, now that we're involved here, we're not so sure that both parties have suffered equally. But I have a proposition; and if you accept it, we'll be happy to withdraw our claim: We'll all get together Mr. Pratt will squirt Mr. Being with a fire extinguisher...and Mr. Being will shoot Mr. Pratt with a gun. Then we'll call it even. And if you don't want to bother with this - well, we're still inclined to take our chances in court."

Little trace remained of the festive atmosphere.

Herman felt he had lost the chance to get out from under his biggest problem. He hated this legal business...On the other hand, some of Grossman's fervor for justice seemed to have rubbed off on him. The old fart certainly had made a point. What kind of wimp would he be to slink out of the fight at this first opportunity?

That son-of-a-bitch Pratt had weaseled him out of a job, insulted Jean, shot him, and then tried to sue him. How much of this was Herman going to take?

This Grossman really was turning out to be a tiger. An old tiger maybe, but what the hell! Why not turn him loose and see what happens?

Despite the great success of his experience with Brahms' *Third*, Herman still remembered his past and sometimes spectacular failures. So it was with some apprehension that he had undertaken the experiment's first official phase. According to Ben's plan, this consisted of simply listening to the works several times. On the one hand, he did not find these initial listenings terribly inspiring; but this is what he had been instructed to expect. On the other hand, maybe because he did not feel pressured for an immediate response, he did find them, for the most part, pleasant.

Sheer, sensual beauty of sound from his new equipment compensated, to a degree, for a feeling that the musical material was somewhat knotty and overlong. And here at home a boring passage was not a liability as it was in the concert hall where he had fallen asleep. Here he could doze off...wake up...no big deal.

Then around the third listening, right on schedule, the great revelation began. Captivating melodies and harmonies materialized from the barrenness of previous listenings. Now, after conscious anticipation, the flowering of his appreciation was nearly as wonderful and beautiful as the music itself.

Some time ago, when Jean had figured out that it was Herman's insecurity about music that nearly ended their relationship, she made clear her unhappiness and her feeling that it was foolish to allow Herman's self conscious musical stumblings to interfere with their affinity for one another. But now that the experiment was working, he felt a great urge to share his excitement with her. It would still be nearly a week before she returned from Europe. At any rate, it was probably better, at least this first time, to follow through on his own, relying on Ben's help. At least she would be back for the actual concert, and he looked forward to sharing that experience with growing anticipation.

Ben stopped over to check on Herman's progress. He asked Herman to give him a brutally honest progress report on his reaction to each piece at that stage - after three listenings.

Tchaikowsky, *Romeo and Juliet*: Some real exciting sections, colorful orchestration and some gorgeous melodies, but too complex and some deadly slow, boring sections. Why didn't Tchaikowsky leave them out and squeeze the excitement and great tunes into a nice compact piece about half as long? Ben suggested that they delay dealing with this until after Herman had read the Shakespeare play.

Mozart, *Piano Concerto*: This was Herman's favorite so far; a beautiful, refined sound. Clearly defined moods, graceful melodies and the last time through he felt that he was developing a sense of balance and architecture in the piece. Ben thought that this sounded fine. Maybe Herman would prefer to deal with this one according to his own instincts, without suggestions. Agreed.

Mahler, *Kindertotenlieder*: This one was for orchestra with mezzo-soprano soloist. At first he had found the soprano disturbing - the strength of the sound and its dramatic urgency were overpowering compared with the popular singers he was used to - but now he felt he was becoming accustomed to this and began to find the stronger, intense sound more interesting. The piece had a lush emotional tone and some beautiful spots, but on the whole it was sort of nebulous and seemed to drag on. Ben asked if Herman knew what the name of the piece meant.

"Yes: Songs on the death of children. And the next question you'll ask me is if I've read the poetry. The answer to that is yes, too. The poems were included in the CD liner notes - beautiful, sorrowful poetry. I read them and then listened to the music, but I don't feel at ease with it yet; the connection between poetry and music is hard for me."

"How long did it take you to read the poetry?"

"About five minutes."

"And how long did the music last?"

"About half an hour."

"Alright," said Ben, "here's what I want you to do: First of all, you have to realize that the great challenge for any composer of vocal music, and therefore the challenge that extends to the listener - is to make the music fit the words; not just the general tone of one to the other, but every stanza, phrase - even down to the word itself might be reflected. It's not enough to simply read the poetry and then listen. Your job as a real listener is to follow every word. The great composers, Mahler among them, drained their minds and souls on this problem and the results are the test of genius.

"Look, these composers weren't mindless talents with an ability to string together pleasant sounds. They were intelligent human beings with fascinating intellects. Now we're not all geniuses, but if you have respect for your own intelligence there's nothing more fascinating than getting in on what they were thinking. It's almost a way to share the creative process, to be in on the miracle of inspiration. A direct connection over centuries, languages and cultures, from Mahler's mind to yours - if you choose to let yourself in on it.

"Look at dogs, for instance. I love dogs. They're nice and furry, they run fast and they've got great ears. But they're not great music lovers. You know why? Nothing upstairs. At least they've got an excuse. For us, though, how we listen is a conscious decision. I'm getting carried away."

"That's okay," said Herman. "I'm getting the point. So tell me specifically how I should apply this to *Kindertoten-lieder.*"

"Well, you can't be lazy. You need to follow the

original language, keep place with the performance, and read the translation simultaneously. This is the only way you can find the full power of music to expand, deepen and intensify a literary experience. You don't need to do this each time you listen; but you've got to do it carefully at least once."

When Ben left, Herman put on the *Kindertotenlieder* and followed the text closely. It was not at all as difficult as he had imagined. The slow pace of the music allowed him to absorb the poetry. He found that there was time to read both languages and that this gave him the sensation of actually understanding the German. More important, he immediately felt a compounded weight of meaning. Passages which had seemed dry now revealed a subtle, radiant significance. It was as though the poetry and music had combined to open a new dimension, fuller and deeper than the sum of the separate elements.

The effect was beyond anything he was prepared for, and he was overcome. He realized that it was no coincidence that Ben had not hung around for this. He began to understand Ben's idea that some artistic experiences can be deeply personal and may not lend themselves well to social events.

Kindertotenlieder was vocal music accompanied by orchestra; not opera, in that it was not staged or acted. Herman had always been so turned off by opera that he had wanted only to avoid it. After his experience with *Kindertotenlieder* his attitude reversed. Whereas before, he considered dramatic singing patently invalid and incredible, he now saw it as a fantastic, multi-dimensional phenomenon, where music invested words and actions with glowing, dreamlike, super-conscious meaning. It occurred to him that it had been foolish to place such importance on simpleminded credibility, that opera could have a deeper validity. He resolved that when his present experiment was over he would begin to explore opera. Doors were opening. He was having a first look at a new world; the immensity was staggering.

When Ben showed up a few nights later, Herman had finished reading Shakespeare's *Romeo and Juliet*. Ben explained that music which refers to an extra-musical concept, such as Tchaikowsky's overture based on Shakespeare's play, is called "program music" as opposed to "pure" or "absolute" music such as the Mozart piano concerto. With program music, as with vocal music, it is the listener's responsibility to find as closely as possible what the composer was attempting to translate into music. Ben asked Herman to identify the essential elements in the story.

They agreed on three: 1) Goodness (embodied by Friar Laurence); 2) Evil (embodied in the feud between the Montagues and the Capulets); 3) Love (Romeo and Juliet). Now they listened to the music, and Ben asked Herman if any connection occurred to him between the main melodies (themes) and the three elements.

They were as clear as day. How could he have missed them before? One complication: the love theme seemed to be in two parts, sometimes separate and sometimes together...of course! Romeo and Juliet apart and united! Herman felt as though he had solved the New York Times crossword puzzle, but better. Tchaikowsky was no dope - genius and ingenious.

Now that Herman had identified the thematic elements,

they listened again. This time Ben instructed him to make a list, not just in his head, but on paper, of the themes and changes both obvious and subtle that marked their various appearances. A logical, organized, complex but clear structure took shape on Herman's paper. Before they were through, Herman had discovered phenomenal detail of expression and a lucid, orderly plot extending from the first note to the last. The passages he had found dull before now appeared profoundly meaningful.

He heard Friar Laurence strumming his harp; he heard the conflict between good and evil, he heard spiritual love of man, innocent yearning, passionate sensual love, anxiety, despair, tragedy, grief, a funeral march, mourning, consolation, repentance, anger and, toward the end, there was no question - he was sure he heard a vision of love transcending earthly existence. It beat the hell out of Drive-in Baby!

Romeo and Juliet, Tchaikowsky
Analysis by Ben and Herman

Time	Introduction
0:00	Slow and hymnlike
	Friar Laurence Theme ("the good") in woodwinds (melody in clarinet)
0:30	Transcedental resolution 3 times slowly with
1:30	harp
2:00	Pizzicatto strings accompany the Friar Laurence theme in woodwinds
3:00	Transcedental resolution again 3 times with harp
4:30	Friar Laurence theme, now agitated, in imitation
5:00	Tension heightens as strings and woodwinds answer
5:30	▬ ▬ ▬ ▬ ▬ ▬ ▬ ▬ ▬
	Main section begins
6:00	**Feud Theme** ("evil") - Fast forceful and driving in full orchestra
6:30	Cellos imitated by piccolo (Feud theme fragments)
	Rushing strings and cymbal crashes
7:00	Feud theme powerful in full orchestra
7:30	Calming
	Love Theme A (Romeo), gently in English horn and violas
8:00	**Love Theme B** (Juliet) sighing in strings
8:30	Romeo theme in strings & Juliet theme in horn now <u>together</u>
9:00	Builds to repeat of love theme
9:30	Quiet passage brings first part gently to close

	Middle section
10:30	Feud theme builds
	Friar Laurence theme in horns
11:30	These two themes in conflict
	Tension builds again
12:30	Powerful Friar Laurence (good) emerges
	triumphant in trumpets
	Last section
13:00	Feud theme returns
13:30	Sighing Juliet theme returns
14:00	Rising waves of sound lead to more and more
14:30	passionate climax of Love themes
15:00	Romeo theme returns questioningly - twice
15:30	Romeo theme again, now in answer
	Feud theme and Friar Laurence theme return
	again in conflict
16:00	Ominous tone emerges in furious low brass
16:30	(death)
	Epilogue
	Funeral march begins in timpani
17:00	Love theme, dirgelike, as a song of mourning
17:30	Hymlike melody in mood of consolation
18:30	Love theme again, transformed now -
	otherworldly (lovers united in death)
19:00	Tragic chords over angry timpani

The plan was that he would work on the Mozart piano concerto by himself. This didn't keep him from using some of the same techniques that worked with the Tchaikowsky. He identified main and subsidiary themes and constructed a chart to help in discovering the structural line. This was a bit more challenging because he had no concrete extra-musical guidelines with which to identify the sounds. Eventually he found that it wasn't necessary to translate musical ideas into words. The musical impressions were frequently difficult or impossible to distill into our greatly more limited verbal language; but the process of focusing attention and keeping track of musical development invariably yielded deeper understanding.

He was intrigued by some references to Mozart's life and character which he found on the notes in the CD package. This led him to read a full biography. Mozart's affection and admiration for Joseph Haydn generated a curiosity in Herman. He would listen to Haydn as soon as he found a chance. Another door was opening.

After his revelations with *Romeo and Juliet* and *Kindertotenlieder* Herman suspected that the Mozart, because of its abstract nature, would not be as effective. He found that he was wrong. It remained his favorite; able to convey ideas and sensations nonetheless real for his inability to completely describe them.

He wondered if different people might be affected differently. Out of curiosity he went to the music library at Lincoln Center and listened to two other recordings of the same concerto, but by different performers. He was just finishing when a very beautiful woman tapped him on the shoulder. She was somewhat older than Herman, probably around forty, with thick black hair in coiled braids.

"Excuse me," she spoke with a slight accent, "I'm sorry to interrupt you, but I was looking for the Mozart "*D Minor Concerto*" and the librarian said you had taken them all. I wonder if I might listen to one while you are using the other."

"Oh sure, as a matter of fact I just finished. You can have both of them."

"May I ask which you found preferable?" she asked. Herman was quick to explain that he was not a musician, but that he did find different strengths in the two performances. He surprised himself by expressing coherent opinions and she, who obviously knew something about music, was interested. They began a pleasant conversation. Having read the record jackets and biography, he did not appear at all ignorant.

He mentioned that he was listening to this concerto in preparation for the Philharmonic concert coming up, and she said that she too was preparing for that concert.

She noticed the diagrams he had been making to keep track of the comings and goings of the various themes in the concerto. He was a little embarrassed.

"Maybe I'm going overboard in being so analytical. My Aunt says that music is to listen to, not to think about."

"Well I think your diagrams are very lovely and a wonderful idea. Mortimer Adler, the philosopher, would be on our side, you know. How would you imagine he defines beauty?"

Herman searched his mind briefly and decided there was nothing in there worth comparing with a real philosopher's definition. "I guess I'd have to give it a lot of thought. What does Adler say?"

"He says beauty is, 'that which pleases upon contemplation.' If we look at a painting, we can focus on individual details and then stand back and view the work as a whole. With sculpture, we can actually touch it. It's all there, complete and at once. Music, however, exists only in time. It's much more difficult to think about, to contemplate, to hold in one's mind, especially in an extended piece which requires that the parts be compared to one another and to the whole, for real understanding - to reveal the full and ultimate beauty. Don't you think so?"

Herman said that he did think so. He really did. He thought how he would enjoy challenging Ben for a definition of beauty and made a note of Adler's, although he was pretty sure he would remember it.

At the same time, it pleased him to be contemplating the considerable beauty of his very interesting new acquaintance.

"It's probably very audacious of me," she said, "but I live just a few blocks away, on Central Park West, and I have there another recording of this concerto that I would love to have you listen to. I really should be embarrassed to ask, but you seem to have such an interest in this piece, and I would really value your opinion."

Herman's brain was whirring. "Is she on the level or is one of those things that always seems to happen to other people finally happening to me? If so, what do I do? Why would I refuse? She certainly has a captivating manner. Well, it's not only her manner. She's captivating all over."

On the way to her apartment he learned that she was born in Rumania, but now lived in Paris and New York. It was obvious that she was well off. It did cross Herman's mind that maybe she would be interested in investing in a computer business, but he dismissed the thought. She was divorced (Uh oh!).

He was both relieved and disappointed that she did have a recording of the concerto and she did seem to be interested in his opinion of it. She asked him to compare it with the other recordings he had heard and listened intently to his comments. On the other hand, he was about to ask her who was playing on the recording when she took off her shoes and sat very close to him on the couch.

She wore one of those blouses with a big floppy collar that stays closed without buttons...unless the wearer moves around or bends over, which she did several times (though not too often for Herman), revealing a luxurious bosom. One of her braids had started to uncoil and dangled provocatively. They had martinis and eventually Herman found himself talking about Jean.

When he caught himself at this, he had a feeling that he had just let himself out of something. Would James Bond have talked about his girlfriend in a situation like this? Not cool. Had it been a Freudian slip? There was a lull in the conversation, and he almost knew what was coming.

"Herman dear, I hope I don't shock you, but as you already know, I am not a shy person and I have a terrible predisposition to be outspoken. I think we are both wondering yes or no. I find you charming, and you have wonderful, sensual lips but you have also a lovely girlfriend, as you told me yourself, and although I am certainly not too old for you, I do think that you may be a little young for me. We have had a lovely afternoon though, haven't we?

And I hope you don't think I led you on too shamefully."

"Shit!" thought Herman. "If this were the movies I would just pull off her clothes and we'd be rolling passionately on the carpet. Sensual lips?...me?"

On his way out she stopped him and said, "As long as I'm being outspoken, I should warn you that you must not stare so intently at a lady's bosom. You must learn to stare more discreetly." She kissed him on the cheek and closed the door behind him. Standing alone in the hall, he could not keep from emitting a loud groan.

In two weeks Herman's leg had healed remarkably. He limped only slightly now. Jean was due back, and he was getting ready to meet her at the airport. As he changed the bandage on his leg he was gratified to see that the scar was still sufficiently nasty-looking to be impressive. The phone rang.

"Hello, Herman? Grossman here."

"Hello Marvin. What's up?"

"Well, I just talked to the other side. They've got a problem. It seems that their guy has been embellishing the truth quite a bit when he talks to them. The more they get into it the less they like it. They're mad as hell at him."

"Well, if they want me to beat him up again, tell them to forget it."

"No, that's not what they had in mind. See, the company's involved, and they'd find it embarrassing to get stuck in court with this. They offered you a twenty five thousand dollar settlement - out of court."

"You're kidding!"

"That's what I told them you'd say. I told them I'd try to talk you into taking Thirty."

"I'll take it! I'll take it!"

"Yeah, well... we're coming out alright on this, but I'll tell you - I would have loved to get that slimy bastard on the stand."

"I was starting to look forward to that myself. But, as it is, that money couldn't come at a better time. I can't believe it! As a matter of fact, I'm going to have to talk to you about helping me set up a new business. And who knows, maybe Pratt will shoot me again. We won't be so easy on him next time, right?"

"Right!"

Herman and Jean had a lot to talk about as they drove from the airport in Herman's rusty station wagon. By the time they were sitting in Herman's apartment, Jean had been brought up to date on all the important developments. Herman ended by explaining how, by putting the settlement money into the new business they could pick up one of those bigger jobs and get a decent start. Herman was already recognized as the leader, the driving force; now he would be the main investor as well.

He said to Jean, "You really lucked out on this, you know? You agreed to marry a wounded, unemployed ignoramus and look how things are shaping up."

"Well I'm not complaining but, according to your own reasoning, that still leaves me with a wounded ignoramus in charge of a new business."

"No, no. There's been a significant falling off in my standing as an ignoramus."

"That's encouraging. What do you base this on?"

"This is the best news of all. You've never met my friend, Ben. He's been helping me out with music. He has a sort of magic formula, based on the effect of repeated listening. We got pretty involved, but the basic principle is simple. it seemed to make sense when we talked about it, but now I've actually been applying the idea as a sort of experiment leading up to this concert that we'll go to on Saturday night - and it's working! It's fantastic. But I don't want to talk about it now. First things first. You wanna see my scar?

The concert did serve, according to plan, as the culmination of the experiment, though in fact Ben's thesis had been thoroughly accepted before this. Each of the pieces had yielded unexpected riches with each listening. Beyond this, Herman realized that what Ben had told him was true: This was just the beginning - he could continue to find new and deeper experiences with these same pieces time and again throughout the years; musical masterpieces are ever-changing.

Whatever it was that he had been seeking when he was moved to look beyond *Drive-in Baby*, he had found - in inexhaustible supply. He had experienced music's dimension of unseen colors, where happiness and sadness are blended in infinite variety, where he could be intimate with the human spirit.

The concert marked the end of Herman's musical self-consciousness in his relationship with Jean, or anybody else for that matter.   He was comfortable as an enthusiastic amateur.   There remained much about music and many pieces yet to learn, but in those pieces that he did know, he had great confidence and felt his judgment to be no less valuable than anyone's.

The concert served to reinforce his new-found confidence in another peculiar way.   The Mozart piano concerto was to end the first half of the program.   As the soloist was greeted by the audience Herman whispered agitatedly to Jean, "My God! I think I know that lady!"

Jean said, "That's no lady, that's Sylva Glantz, one of the greatest pianists in the world."

"Remember that lady I told you about from the library? That's her, I'd swear it!"

"You're kidding!   How could you have been in her apartment and not known who she was?"

"I never asked," said Herman.   "I told you, we just had a discussion about music...and I had to leave in a hurry."

Though somewhat shaken, he found the performance of the Mozart particularly moving.   Evidently he was not alone, as the audience responded with an unusually enthusiastic and sustained ovation.

During the bows and applause following the concerto Jean asked, "What do you suppose this is?" and showed him an almost blank half-page in the program.   It said, printed in large letters:

HERMAN DEAR:

YOU MUST STOP AND SAY HELLO BEFORE LEAVING TONIGHT

YOUR FRIEND FROM THE LIBRARY

Immediately after the concert they found their way backstage where a small crowd had gathered around the pianist. She greeted Herman with an embrace...and Jean as well, saying, "Herman has told me about you." Turning to Herman again, "Did you realize the recording I played for you was my own of several years ago? Your comments had a rare honesty. I took them very much to heart, and it is largely thanks to you that my performance tonight was especially satisfying to me."

She continued, turning to Jean, "I recognized as soon as I spoke to him that he has a rare and unspoiled artistic insight. He is a treasure. You are a fortunate girl. And he has such lovely lips!"

About the Author

Dr. Robert Danziger holds a Ph.D. in music from New York University. He is currently a member of the music faculty at California State University, Stanislaus where his music appreciation courses are much in demand. He has served as Chairman of the Music Department at the University of Bridgeport in Connecticut. A new book by Dr. Danziger, "The Revelation of Music - Learning to Love the Classics" has recently been published by Jordan Press.

About The Musical Ascent of Herman Being
by Robert Danziger

What the students said:

- A fantastic learning experience. I really enjoyed this book.
- An insightful book. This book kept me awake.
- A practical guide to music with a touch of comedy, drama, mystery and romance. The ending was great.
- Entices the reader into a deeper, more sophisticated involvement with music.
- Hysterically funny.
- Brings the reader a true understanding of classical music.
- Delightful, innovative: And it works.
- The story was something I could relate to.
- Easy to read and yet not simple minded.
- A thoughtful. creatively written aid to entering the world of art music.
- It made me laugh.
- A sneaky way to get a point across. I recommend this book to everyone.
- Not the average textbook. It kept my interest and I seem to retain more information.
- Colorful and truly fun to read.
- It is everything the cover says it is (a rare accomplishment).
- Quick reading and easy to understand.
- A witty book which restores faith to the depressed music listener.
- This reading made the class worth enrolling in.

Among the Colleges and Universities Using
The Musical Ascent of Herman Being

Alaska Pacific University
Albright College
Arizona State University
Ashland Community College
Augustana College
Aurora University
Barton College
Bergen Comm. College
Bethel College
Bluffton College
Boise State University
Bradford College
Bradley University
Bridgewater State College
Bucknell University
Caldwell College
Cal State, Hayward
Cal State, Dominguez Hills
Cal State, Stanislaus
Cal State, Sacramento
Cal State San Jose
Cañada College
Calvin College
Catawba College
Cayuga Cnty. Comm. College
Central College
Central State University
Chautauqua Institution
Centre College of Kentucky
Chautauqua Institution
Clark University
Coker College
College of Idaho
College of Saint Rose
College of San Matteo
College of Wooster
Columbia Basin College
Covenant College
Cuayahoga Community College
Culver-Stockton College
Dakota State University
Dawson College
Dekalb College
DePaul University
DePauw University
Diablo Valley College
Dixie College

Earlham College
Elmhurst College
Emanuel College
Essex Community College
Eureka College
Florida International University
Floyd College
Fort Lewis College
Frederick Community College
Furman College
George Fox College
Georgia Southern College
Georgia State University
Gettysburg College
Georgia State University
Grossmont Cuyamoca College
Gustavus Adolphus College
Hartnell College
Hesston College
Hope College
Illinois State University
Indian Hills Community College
Indiana University
James Madison University
Keene State College
Keystone Jr. College,
Lebanon Valley College
Lehigh University
Limestone College
Lindenwood College
Lincoln Memorial University
Lock Haven College
Los Medanos College
Louisiana College
Lourdes College
Lynchburg College
Marshall University
Martin Methodist College
McNees State University
Mesa College
Miami University
Michigan Christian College
Middle Tennessee State U.
Midwestern State University
Mississippi State University
Modesto Jr. College
Montana State University

Montclair State College
Moraine Valley College
Moorehead State University
National University
Nazareth College
Nebraska Wesleyan University
New Mexico State University
North Central University
Northern Michigan University
Northwest College
Northwest Community College
Notre Dame College
Ohio Wesleyan University
Olympic College
Oxnard College
Pacific Union College
Paris Jr. College
Pennsylvania State University
Peru State College
Porterville College
Potomax State College
Providence College
Quincy College
Radford University
Randolph Macon College
Reed College
Rice University
Rutgers University
San Diego Mesa College
Santa Barbara Comm. College
Santa Clara University
Shippensburg University
Shoreline Community College
Sioux Falls College
Skyline College
Snow College
Southeastern College
Southwest State U, MN
Southern Utah State College
St Ambrose University
St. Gregory's College
St. Lawrence University
St. Mary's College, CA
St. Mary's College, IN
St. Mary's College, NE
St. Mary's College. TX
St. Mary's University, TX
St. Xavier College
Stephen F Austin State U.
Teikyo Marycrest University
Thiel College
Tulane University

Tusculum College
University of Alabama
University of Arizona
University of Arkansas
University of Bridgeport
University of Chattanooga
University of Colorado
University of Delaware
University of Houston
University of Montana
University of Nebraska
University of Nevada
University of North Carolina
University of Rhode Island
University of San Diego
University of South Carolina
University of Southern Colorado
University of Southern Utah
University of St. Thomas
University of Tennessee
University of the Ozarks
University of Utah
University of Southern Colorado
University of Virginia
University of Western Florida
University of Wisconsin
University of Wyoming
Utah State University
Valpariso University
Vermillion Community College
Vernon Regional Jr. College
Victor Valley College
Virginia Intermont College
Virginia Wesleyan College
VIrginia Tech
Waldorf College
Wake Forest University
Wayne State College
Weber State University
Wenatchee Community College
West Virginia Wesleyan Univ.
Westfield State College
Windward Community College
William Woods College
Yakima Valley Comm. College

What the professors say about
The Revelation of Music.

"Excellent! Concise, and all the important aspects of musical enjoyment highlighted. Thanks for writing a book the non-musician can use, and not another history book."
Professor Jeff Meyers, Itawamba Community College.

"Revelation is the book I've been searching for to use in my general education. music appreciation class."
Professor Karen Schwartz, Victor Valley College.

. . . gives more detail without being overwhelming."
Professor C.B Rhinehart, Virginia Intermont College.

"I am very impressed with the content, flexibility and humor of The Revelation of Music."
Professor Frank Archer, Caldwell College.

"I really like the concise, open-ended approach of Revelation..."
Professor David Hendrickson, Tusculum College.

". . . what we need for 'Intro to Music' - a book that is not too technical yet interesting."
Professor Sr. Anita Marchasseault, Notre Dame College.

"Very readable."
Professor Mary Dave Blackman, Weber State University.

"The explanation on opera is insightful and accessible to the amateur."
Professor Diana Greuninger, Weber State University."

The Revelation of Music - **Learning to Love the Classics.** Presenting a thorough, non-technical introduction, this book includes unique, practical suggestions for experiencing art music. This new Revised and Enlarged Edition comes packed with a 70 minute CD with recordings of selected masterpieces and digitally indexed listening guides.

<u>Partial Contents</u>
An approach to Listening * Materials of Music * Instruments * The Orchestra * Instrumental Forms * Opera * Voices * Vocal forms * Styles * Composers * Recordings and Stereo Equipment * Concertgoing * Historically Authentic Performances * Digitally Indexed Listening Guides

5½x8½*340 pages*Quality Paperback
ISBN 0-9613427-7-3
Jordan Press*$24.95

Order Form
To: Jordan Press,
620 Sycamore Avenue
Modesto, CA 95354
(Phone: 209 571-2030)

Please rush me _____ copies of "The Revelation of Music - Learning to Love the Classics" @ $24.95 each, plus $2.00 for postage. Payment enclosed.

Name _____

Address _____